S0-ARM-545

My Dirty Thirties

Male/Female/Male

My Dirty Thirties

Male/Female/Male

Kelly Carr

New Tradition Books

My Dirty Thirties: Male/Female/Male
by
Kelly Carr

New Tradition Books
ISBN 1932420304
All rights reserved
Copyright © 2004 by Kelly Carr
This book may not be reproduced in whole or in part without
written permission.

*This book is a work of fiction. Names, characters, places and
incidents are either the product of the author's imagination or are
used fictitiously. Any resemblance to actual events or locales or
persons, living or dead is entirely coincidental.*

For information contact:
New Tradition Books
newtraditionbooks@yahoo.com

For the women in their thirties.

Toe-curling good.

"Whenever you're ready, Katrina," Wes said.

Whenever I was ready... Whenever *I* was ready. It was up to me. They were waiting on me. They wouldn't move until I told them to move. A sense of power, of pure unadulterated power, washed over me just then. It was good to know that I was calling the shots. I was in total control and it made me feel like the most special woman in the world. And the mightiest. Right then and there, I was the only woman in the world to them.

My eyes turned to Wes and then to the Zack. I couldn't help but grin mischievously. I was so naughty. The thought of what we were about to do was making me feel like a bad, bad girl. It was good to be so bad. Especially in this case and especially with these two men who sat patiently waiting for me to do what I was going to do.

They wouldn't even move until I told them to!

Like good little boys, they sat at the foot of my bed, each keeping their distance from the other as their eyes devoured me and my skimpy outfit. Their eyes were all over me, penetrating me, almost making me *feel* their stares. I was dressed in a tight black tube-top and a short denim mini-skirt. My heels were nearly four inches off the floor and pushed into a pair of clear plastic stripper platform shoes, which had been a gift from Wes. The tube-top had come from Zack and the miniskirt was from my own closet. We had dressed me tonight, each of us picking out our favorite article of clothing.

I wasn't wearing any underwear.

I knew I looked like a total slut. But I liked looking that way. My make-up was heavy and my long, dark hair was curled and piled on top of my head. I looked good, for a slut. I looked real good. They loved the way I looked. I could tell from the way they stared at me.

The main reason I liked the outfit was because I didn't normally dress like this. Not at all. I was usually a very conservative dresser but this was their preferred outfit. I wore it to please them and to please myself. But mainly I wore it because it was short, it was skimpy and therefore, it allowed for easy access. It was the kind of outfit a man wanted to rip off a woman's body—with her permission, of course. It was the kind of outfit that made their mouths water and their skin tingle and their dicks stir. It didn't take much imagination to visualize what was beneath the clothes. Their hands could find their way easily underneath to grope me. And it could come off in seconds.

There they were. Two of them. One. Two. One plus one is two. Plus one is three. There were three of us. Three of us getting geared up for our next threesome, our next foray into the magical world of group loving. Into our next excursion of sinful delights that would leave me panting and begging for more and fantasizing about our next time, about when we would do it again. And I wouldn't be satisfied until it occurred and then, when it was over, I would want it again and again.

They were still waiting on me to make the first move. Both of them. My men. *My* men. Waiting on me to give them the cue. Waiting on me to seduce them with my mind and with my soul, but mostly with my body. I felt like such a goddess then. It was such an addictive feeling.

I smiled at both of them, quite sure of myself, quite sure of them, and got out of my chair. I took my time walking over. I took my time to study them, like the way they studied me. I knew they liked with they saw. Knowing that gave me power to move forward, power to quicken my pace. They liked my face and my blue eyes. They liked the freckles across my nose and they liked my plump red lips. They liked my petite but strong body. They liked my breasts which were squeezed into the tube-top but spilling over, inviting them to take a good look and tempting them into taking a good feel, then they could suck them, grope them and pleasure me. They liked my legs which looked longer in the heels and gave them more curve then they already possessed and they possessed quite a bit. They liked all of me and I liked all of them.

Their eyes were all over my body, then, as if they couldn't get enough of it, of me, as if they were fearful that it might suddenly disappear without them getting the best look they could. Their eyes skimmed it before they concentrated on a leg or a cheek or a lip before they began to scan it again. They didn't want to miss anything. Men are such visual creatures. I loved giving them the visual they wanted. I loved being their pin-up girl, their sex goddess, their one and only.

Wes smiled at me. The corners of his intense blue eyes crinkled a little when he smiled. He was so handsome, so unbelievably handsome with dark hair and olive skin and a sharply defined jaw-line. He was dressed in a blue button down shirt and a pair of black slacks. He always dressed like that. He always took care with the way he dressed and always shaved for me. He was a handsome man who was made more handsome by his great personality. He knew how to make me smile and he knew when to let me talk. But mostly, he knew when to hold me and when to let me go.

Zack didn't look so bad himself. He was lighter than Wes, his hair was dirty blond and he it wore purposefully messed up. He had a goatee and nice, masculine lips I loved to nibble at whenever he was around me. He was tall and he was strong. His shoulders were wide and his arms big. He was a good guy and was better than most I'd met.

They were both so wonderful. I don't know how I ended up with them, but I wasn't about to ask any questions, lest I tempted fate. I would not, could not screw this up. It was the best situation a woman could find herself in. I knew a good thing when I saw it and so I accepted it, as they accepted me.

They were motionless at the foot of the bed, sitting still, waiting on me to make the first move. I continued to walk slowly and allowed them to devour me with their eyes. That look they gave me, powered by lust, gave me a surge of energy. It was so nice to be wanted in this way.

I would think of nothing else from this moment on other than what they were doing to my body and what I doing for theirs. It was time to get the show on the road. I couldn't take the suspense any longer. I was about to jump out of my skin from all the excitement, from all the anticipation. No formalities were needed. We all knew what we were here to do and we were all here to take care of me. It was totally selfish but that made it all the more divine.

As I neared them, Wes got out of his chair and stood, taking me into his arms. He began to kiss me softly and slowly, really taking his time to get my juices flowing. He didn't have to bother. I had been hot for this all day. I had fantasized about it at work and while I was taking my bath and while I was dressing and at dinner. I had thought about nothing since the last time we did it, besides thinking about when we would do it again.

Wes bent me back and began to suck at my throat. A deep moan came out of my lips and my pulse quickened. That was Zack's cue to join in. He came up behind me and bent down behind me, running his hands over my ass, running them up my skirt until he was playing with my pussy. I was so wet I was dripping. He began to gnaw at me. I shuddered as he began to bite at my legs. It was coming and it was coming strong and it was coming to take me over. It was that good feeling that was entrenched in my body and begging for release.

But not until I said so. I was totally in control. They were my stud boys, my men, they did what *I* wanted. I called all the shots. Neither looked at the other as they both began to paw at me with their big hands. They acted as if the other wasn't in the room. They never acknowledged each other's presence except for a friendly handshake before and polite goodbye after. They weren't there for each other. They were there for me, to give me pleasure. It was about me, not about them. They were there to pleasure me and me only.

I pushed Wes back onto the bed and got between his legs, standing. In a second flat I had his pants unzipped and was bent over him. I grabbed his dick and began to give him head, using a little pressure at first, which was what he liked best. As I sucked him, Zack got behind me and tore the skirt from my body and then he was sucking at me—at my pussy—like I sucked at Wes. *Ohhhhh, Goodddd!* Wes held my head as I went up and down on his hard cock. It throbbed slightly and I knew I was doing too good a job. If I kept it up, if I sucked any harder, he would come. And I wasn't ready for that. The night was early and we'd just gotten started.

I ground my pussy against Zack's face for a moment before I stopped and jerked my head towards the side. He grinned and went and lay down across the top of the bed positioning himself so he could take me. I laid on my side beside him with my back to him and then Wes was in front of me, making me the meat of the sandwich. They were both at me, taking me, taking all I had to offer and I had a lot. Their hands were all over my body and Wes jerked the tube-top down and began to suck on my breasts. He moaned and grunted a little as he did so. I loved that sound coming out of his mouth, coming from deep inside him. I stared at Zack over my shoulder and loved the way he was playing with my pussy with one hand. He slid it in sideways, opening up my ripe lips, and then bent down to lick at my neck. I turned over to Zack and he totally took over my pussy. He kissed his way down my body and pushed open my legs and began to lick and suck at it. He did that so well. He gave perfect head. But then again, so did Wes.

But right now, Wes was sucking on my tits as Zack sucked on my pussy. A sharp moan escaped my lips and I threw my head back as all these sensations took me over. I felt the first little orgasm; it was on its way. I moaned and a grunt came out from inside me and I pressed myself onto his face, grinding. I could help myself. I was done in. I was coming, bucking up off the bed as I came and I began to purr as it dissipated then went away.

The best part came next.

I turned to Wes and opened my legs wider and he got between them, his hard cock pointing at me. I grabbed onto it and stroked it and then helped him put it in. I almost gasped. He was good-sized man, his dick had to be at least eight long and hard inches and it took up every square inch of my pussy as he shoved it in.

Zack moved until his cock was in my face. I grabbed onto it and began to suck with all of my might as Wes fucked me. He gasped and pulled back a little. I slowed down and gave it a lighter suck, which he liked and nodded with approval. I winked at him and then I began to feel another orgasm, this one much bigger. When I was this turned on, I could come at the drop of a hat but I knew if I prolonged it, I could have a bigger one, an intense one that came from deep down inside me and erupted slowly. Those were the best. I wanted one of those, so I grabbed onto Wes and slowed him down a little. He slowed and bent to suck at my tits. I threw my head back and went back to concentrating on Zack's cock. I sucked and stroked it until I tasted his precum.

I pulled back a little just as Wes began to pound me harder. I was going to come sooner than expected if he kept it up. But I couldn't control myself. If I didn't focus on it, I might lose it, and I didn't want that. So I forgot about everything else as it began to play with me, tease me. It was coming just like I wanted it to. I shouldn't ignore it. I gave myself over to it and a slight scream tore out of my throat as it hit me and it hit me hard, so hard I was bucking up against Wes and nearly grunting in my passion. I couldn't get enough then. I couldn't get enough of the moment or of my passion or of them. *Them.* I loved them both.

That was their cue to get things in motion. It didn't take Wes long to come and he was coming hard. It was still tickling me, the orgasm. A funny little squeak erupted from my lips and my toes began to curl as I was being fucked, as I fucked back as Zack was pumping into my mouth then and all of a sudden, I exploded with another orgasm. I came and it came at me in spurts: one, two, and three. I shook with each spurt and Zack came just then, came in my mouth and I sucked him dry as I came and then I felt the last of Wes's cum exploding inside my body.

I shuddered. It was over. My eyes fluttered open and then I smiled at both of them. They smiled back. We smiled with satisfaction. There's nothing like good sex. Nothing. I never believed life could be so wonderful. It's good to be wrong about a few things, but I knew one thing for sure. I was one lucky bitch.

My dirty thirties.

I know what you're thinking. Well, maybe I don't. Regardless, let me set the record straight. I never thought I would be in a relationship with one good man, let alone two. I never thought I would ever be involved in a male/female/male threesome nor did I think that I would get off on it so much. Like most people, I thought those threesomes were not only about the woman getting off but about the men getting off as well—*with each other.* Not appealing to me, to say the least, but if that's your bag, then that's your bag. But that's not what this story is about.

Not to say that I didn't have any preconceptions about three-ways, either. When I was younger I did, but then I watched a few pornos and realized that, no, that wasn't the way it worked at all. It was all about the woman and her pleasure. Sure the guys got pleasure too, but *not* from one another. They got it from the woman. And the woman, in this case, was me. *Me.* I loved that. There was so much sexual power in it. Yeah, power. To know that I could say who, what, when, where and how and they'd oblige was the best feeling in the world. It was beyond bliss. It was downright addicting.

It's all really dirty. Not dirty in a bad way but dirty in a good way. Dirty because it feels good to be so damn bad and to get *off* on it. Dirty is a good word. A very, very good word.

I loved that *I* was the one both of them wanted and that they saw me as this totally sexual creature. They knew that I would do anything to sustain and sate my passions. My passions. Sounds a little soap opera-ish, but, hey, that's the right word in this case. A few years ago, I wouldn't have even thought I had anything like passions to worry about. I was just trudging along, living my life like anyone else and not really concerned about sex or getting off. Now it's all I think about. It just started one day, right out of the blue. One day, it was like I didn't care about sex and the next, I *really* cared about it.

Well, it happened right after I turned thirty. I like to call it "The Thing".

And boy did The Thing happen. It was like I was suddenly awake. It was like I was suddenly alive. I just began to quiver all over. I awoke from a fog and felt such sexual energy that I began to tingle, just tingle with the thought of doing it. It was hard to contain it, too. I just had to start having sex all the time. I began to feel really, really…well, horny. Sure, I had sex before all this and I enjoyed it, but to be honest, I could live without it. I rarely fantasized and I didn't even masturbate. Now I do it all the time. Sometimes even when my boys are watching. They love to watch me play with myself and then they race each other to the bed to see which one gets me first.

When I hit my thirties, I began to feel really sexual and horny all the time. I call it my dirty thirties. I wouldn't go back to my twenties for nothing now. I was a bore in my twenties and bordering on being a prude. Now I couldn't imagine going without sex even though when I was younger, I went without it quite a bit. That may have been what led to my divorce. But looking back on it, I suppose we had good sex. He seemed to enjoy it anyway.

Oh, yeah, my divorce. I am, as they say, a divorcée. I came to Las Vegas with my then-husband, Tony. He had gotten a job at one of the casinos doing some logistical thing. We left our small, hometown Tennessee town with a U-Haul and some pretty big dreams.

Once we got to Vegas, Tony began to work these really long hours. Well, that's what he told me. He did work a lot, but he was also partaking in the delights of Vegas. He was partying his ass off and kicking up his heels and generally having a good time. Without me.

Not that he didn't ask me to join him occasionally. He did. He'd say, "Hey, a bunch of us are going out to a club. Meet me there." Sounded nice, but there were things to do like setting our house up and looking for a job. Once I landed a little gig as a receptionist at an insurance company, I didn't feel like partying after the long hours I was putting in. The bosses at the insurance company were slave drivers and, being the people pleaser I once was, I thought I had to put up with their shit. So I did.

I did feel resentment that Tony was out having a good time while I was working my ass off and we got into a bunch of fights over it. But he told me, "Look, this is why we moved here. Besides, I have to make contacts and be available. That's part of my job now."

So I let it go. I guess Tony got tired of asking me to join him because after a while, the invitations stopped. I didn't notice nor did I care much as I was usually exhausted after I got home from work. It didn't really matter to me what time he came home as long as he *came* home. I, being the good little stay-at-home woman with a full time job, let him enjoy himself. Besides we had been married forever so I never suspected he would cheat and if he did, I never suspected it would mean anything.

Nevertheless, when he found his true calling as a party animal and decided to leave me, I was somewhat devastated. No, I was beside myself. I think I cried for a month straight. *What am I going to do without him?* Blah, blah, blah. And it just seemed to come out of nowhere. One day we were married and the next, he wanted a divorce. The question of why was stamped on my brain. I couldn't get past it. I was hung-up on "why". *Why did he do this to me? Why wasn't I good enough? Why was this happening? Why all of a sudden? Why doesn't he love me anymore? Why? Why? Why? Why?* I thought if I could understand why then we could work it out. But it doesn't work like that.

I remember saying to him, "But *why?*"

He just stared at me, looking sadder than I felt. "I don't know, but I just want to be free for a while. It's really not you, honey."

But it felt like me. It felt like I had done something wrong. Something terrible. Why else would he want out? However, there was nothing I could do about it. Yeah, I have to admit I did all the necessary begging and pleading but that didn't hold him. Because we'd married so young, he wanted to sow his wild oats. It was as simple as that and looking back on it, I understand. Who could blame him? There was nothing I could do. Not one damn thing because when one person wants out of a marriage, there's nothing for the other one to do but step aside. If you're lucky, it will only hurt for a little while. Most of us aren't that lucky. I hurt for nearly six full months. But after that, I was okay. I was okay because in the midst of all this awful pain, I began my transformation.

After the divorce, I was awarded alimony because we'd been together for over ten years. Tony didn't like that much, but then again, he'd been the one to initiate the divorce and there wasn't a damn thing he could do but pay. I was also awarded our house and most of the furniture. Not that I reveled in it or anything. I was lonely and if Tony had wanted to come back to me, I would have welcomed him with open arms.

It was hell living without him. I felt all alone in

this new, bigger city and even considered moving back home. I stopped going to work and lost my job. I lay around the house and did nothing but flip the channels on the TV. But being miserable gets *old* after a while. Sure, misery loves company, but I was tired of being its buddy.

One morning I woke up early, looked around my bedroom at all the boxes that still needed to be unpacked and felt... I felt like unpacking them. They had been there for months, ever since we'd bought the house. I was tired of stumping my toes on them and I was tired of their staid, ugly brown appearance. I wanted those boxes out of my life.

I got up out of bed and went to the boxes, tore them open and started to sort through the junk. I decided most of it was crap and that I should just throw it away. I picked up the box, took it outside and put it on the curb. I stared at the box, sitting there and I felt satisfaction. I felt like I had accomplished something. It was a good feeling so, I turned on my heel and went back inside and went through the entire house. I moved junk around and tore through boxes and closets until I had the entire house almost emptied and sitting outside in the driveway waiting for the garbage men.

After I had delivered the last box out of the house, I noticed something odd. There was a woman going through the boxes. She caught me staring at her, jerked and smiled like she was embarrassed. I couldn't help but smile back. What the hell was she doing?

"Hey, are you having a yard sale?" she asked.

I just stared at her and shrugged. "I guess."

"You got a lot of stuff here," she said.

"Mostly junk."

"Oh, no, it's good stuff."

It was?

"How much do you want for this?" she asked and held up an old vase *I'd* bought at a yard sale.

"I dunno," I said. "A dollar?"

"For this?" she asked. "You know its milk glass, don't you?"

I didn't. I knew I hated it and wanted to get rid of it for years but Tony liked it and told me to hold onto it. But Tony wasn't here now, was he? No. And I could sell the damn thing for a dollar if I wanted to. In fact, most of this shit I'd kept because of Tony, who was the world's biggest packrat. Now I could get rid of it all! And there were all kinds of shit in the garage he said he'd pick up. It had been there since the divorce. Why not get rid of that, too? It was the best idea I'd had in years.

"Cool," she said and smiled. "I'll take it."

"Okay," I said, not sure what the hell was going on.

Just then, a car drove up, stopped and an older couple got out and immediately began to sort through the boxes. I just stood there and when they asked how much something was, I told them. After everybody dispersed, I had about twenty bucks in my pocket. I looked down at myself. I was still in my pajamas.

I ran inside the house, changed into a pair of jeans and a t-shirt and ran back out. There were about five people going through the boxes now. I smiled widely. This was going to be a good day.

I worked all day on selling my old crap. By two o'clock, I had made almost a thousand bucks off my impromptu yard sale. I could afford a new couch! And maybe some new pots and pans. I could change my life by changing my surroundings.

A middle-aged man asked me, "Are you moving?"

"Uh, no," I said and smiled at him.

He eyed me. "Oh, I just though if you had any furniture you wanted to sell…"

Boy, did I ever. I hated my furniture. I hated the old couch and the ugly coffee table and my cheap dining room set. I decided it had to go, all of it.

"You can have a look," I said and jerked my head to the front door. "If you see anything you want, let me know."

He smiled at me and went inside the house just as a woman pushed a wad of cash in my hand.

"That's for this," she said and pointed to two boxes.

I nodded. "Okay, thanks!"

She left and was replaced by a little girl who held up an old teddy bear that Tony had given me for Valentine's years ago.

"How much is this?" she asked sweetly.

"For you," I said and bent down to her eye level. "It's free."

She smiled and thanked me, then skipped over to her mother. I wished I had a better teddy bear to give her than that old thing, but she seemed to like it.

The man came out of the house and said, "I'll give you a couple a thousand for it all."

No way! I couldn't believe my luck! My mouth

dropped. "You will?"

He nodded.

I said hurriedly, not giving him time to change his mind, "I'll take it. When can you get it?"

"I can have a truck here in a few hours," he said. "I own a used furniture shop."

So that was that.

I worked all afternoon and into the night. The people just kept coming and buying all my old crap. I guess everyone loves a yard sale. The man came back with a big truck and he and two other guys took all my furniture. After they left, I began to pick up trash from the lawn and pack the rest of the crap up into garbage bags. Another man came up to me and told me he would take the rest of it for fifty bucks. I was so relieved that I was going to get rid of the rest of it, I readily agreed.

It was about nine that night before I realized that all I had to eat all day was a banana and a coke. I was starving. I went inside and ordered a pizza, got myself a beer and took a tour through my now nearly empty house.

As I walked through the house, I smiled. It was such a relief to be rid of all that crap. I had cleaned it out and now I could start over. I stopped walking and stood taller. It, just then, occurred to me. I was going to start over; I was really going to start afresh. I was going to *move on.*

Wow. Tony really wasn't here with me anymore. It suddenly hit me. I was alone. But being alone meant I would never have to pick up after him again! I would never have to "remind" him to mow the yard or to clean up his messes. I would never have to worry about him pissing me off by not helping out around the house ever again!

I was free.

I threw my arms open and ran through the house. I was free! It was then that I realized that being married really hadn't been that great. It was kinda a pain in the ass to be honest. I stopped and thought about it. Many times I had felt like I was the one suffocating, wanting out. But when you're married, you work through that crap, even if you don't want to. Tony had actually done me a favor! I was free and I could do whatever I wanted. I didn't have to worry about reporting to someone again. I didn't have to worry about shit. I was free, free, *free!*

I grinned to myself and walked into the empty bedroom. I didn't have a bed anymore. That made me smile because if that was my biggest problem, then I was doing alright.

Mourning time, over.

The next morning, I awoke in my sleeping bag that had somehow escaped the yard sale and I felt different. I realized something was missing in my life and it wasn't just all the junk I had sold at the yard sale. And, like the junk, it wasn't something I wanted, either. I realized that the pain was gone. I was finally over Tony. I didn't care if he wanted to come back now. As a matter of fact, he could kiss my ass. I didn't want him after all that shit he put me through. My mourning time was over.

I danced around my bedroom for a few minutes after I had my breakthrough. I shook my ass and felt alive. I was so happy. I hadn't felt this good in *years*. I danced around the room and made it to the bathroom where I picked up my toothbrush and danced some more. I danced until I caught myself in the mirror.

Oh, good God.

I stopped, turned to the mirror and my mouth fell open. Was that me? I shook my head and opened my eyes wider. It was me. And I was fat! No wonder Tony had left me! I had to be at least forty pounds overweight. I looked terrible. I had rolls of fat hanging off me and, dear Lord! I had back fat! I had never had back fat before in my life but I had it now! How long had I let myself go and why had I done it? Well, depression will do that sort of thing. Also, eating vats of chocolate to ease the pain doesn't help matters.

I guess I hadn't noticed I was getting fat because I had stopped caring about myself. And I had avoided mirrors like the plague. But now I couldn't avoid it any longer. As I stared at myself, I realized I used to look pretty good but now I looked like... I looked like a bitter divorcée. I looked like a woman who didn't give a shit about herself.

I had dark circles under my eyes. My face looked blotchy from too much caffeine and sugar. That's all I ate, that's what I lived on. I didn't care about myself and I abused my body because of my misery. And now it pissed me off. I was so pissed off at myself for letting myself go, I could have spit. Why had I done that? Over a man? Sure, he had been the love of my life, but did that mean I had to basically deny my existence once we were done? No, it didn't.

I took a stand. Right then, I took a stand to better myself. Tony might have left me but that didn't mean I had to live like this. I didn't have to be overweight. I didn't have to have blotchy skin. And I didn't have to wear frumpy clothes. Frumpy clothes…?

I raced to my closet. Oh, dear Lord! It looked like the closet of a grandmother on her way to her Florida retirement home! I didn't have dresses hanging in there, I had tents! I needed new clothes, a whole new wardrobe. But why should I buy a new wardrobe for this body? I didn't like my body; I didn't like all the fat on it. I had to change it first.

When had I decided to stay fat? I thought about it. Well, I knew I had gained about five pounds a year for every year I'd been married. We'd been married almost ten. Fifty pounds! I was at least fifty pounds overweight! Surely that couldn't be right.

It was right. I weighed almost 174 pounds. I jumped off the scale as if it had bitten me. *When did this happen?*

And just what the hell was wrong with me? I had acted like once I was married my life was over. I had turned into my mother! Oh, God, that was my worse fear! My mother was miserable! She hated her life. She was fat. She told me I shouldn't move to Vegas.

I didn't have to be like my mother. I could change. I could do it. I didn't have anything to lose, did I? Nothing to lose but this fat off my body. Nothing to lose but the misery.

I made the decision that I was going to change my life. I didn't ask for this. I didn't ask for my husband to leave me. I didn't ask to be alone. I didn't ask to be fat. I was going to change it all. Everything in my life was going to be better. I was tired of being tired. I was sick of feeling bad, of being miserable. And I was going to do something about it. And it started on that day.

I looked around the bedroom. I really needed to buy a bed. After that, I'd get started on all the other stuff.

I was nervous and embarrassed when I went to the gym for the first time but, oddly enough, the people who worked there were nice. I had expected them to be assholes because they were skinny and in good shape. They set me up on an exercise program and even told me what to eat to lose weight.

I got hooked on exercising and would go to the gym nearly every day. Something just overcame me and I couldn't help but go along with it. In a few months time, my weight was down and I was getting in great shape. I was still overweight and I had a long way to go, but I was determined. I even became friends with the people who worked there. I also became friendly with the other people like myself who were trying to get in shape. The owner of the gym noticed how well I got along with them and offered to send me to a fitness instruction class so I could work for him. So, in addition to a new body, I got a new career. And one that paid a lot more than I was making being a receptionist.

It didn't stop there. Why should it? A new body deserves a new wardrobe. I had put it off for a long time but the day finally came. I emptied my closet, cringing at all the sad mistakes I'd made when I was unhappy. Or, rather, when I didn't care what I looked like. I had a freakin' dress jumpsuit in there! It was a onesie! I had a onesie! And it was a floral print!

Out, out, out. It all went into the garbage. As I was purging my closet, I was purging my soul, getting rid of all that crap in there that brought me down and made me miserable. No more! No more unhappy, lonely nights! No more knit pants! No more crying myself to sleep! No more being the victim.

I was a new woman. And I got a new wardrobe to go with along with it. I went out and spent a small fortune on new clothes. I bought only hip and stylish things and if they happened to cost a little bit more, then so be it. I'd never spent money on myself before but the times were changing. I was changing into a new woman who was going to live a new life and she *had* to have some new clothes to go along with it.

I refurnished my house and only bought things I liked. It was nice to not have to get someone else's opinion, too. I bought hip, stylish furniture and new mirrors and pictures for the walls. After I was done, I had one groovy pad that included a crushed blue velvet couch and a light blue shag rug. I was also in debt, which meant I had to work a lot of overtime, but I now had the kind of home I'd always wanted.

I started going out at night, hitting clubs with my friends from the gym. Men hit on me left and right. It was great. I was having the time of my life. I was suddenly happy. I was glad Tony had divorced me; otherwise, I wouldn't have known the joy of being able to flirt with other men. I wouldn't have known how good it felt to be free. Maybe Tony had been onto something. Besides, he was out having the time of his life, so why shouldn't I?

It's like this. They say things happen for a reason, right? Something bad happens but then, hey, life goes on and so did mine. I kissed my ex goodbye and took a class in fitness instruction, got a pretty good job and then all of a sudden, I'm in demand. Success was mine for the taking. All of a sudden, I had a client base that grew almost daily. It felt so good to know people wanted me to help them get in shape. People are always talking about how I transformed their bodies and their attitudes. I made a difference in people's lives. Me! Before I couldn't even help myself but after this one bad thing happened, my world opened up.

So I had this great job and I loved it. I loved pushing people to get their asses in shape and I loved the adrenaline rush from a hard workout. I made a good living doing it, too, and in addition to the alimony I got from Tony, I have a nice little life. I would get up early, go to work and after work, I would go out with some of the girls and hit the clubs. As I said, I had married young and had never really experienced single life before and I can tell you, I loved it.

And the men loved me. They loved my firm little body and my long brown hair and my blue eyes. They loved my southern accent and would always get me to "talk" for them. "Say y'all," they'd beg me. "Alright, y'all," I'd say and shake my head. "That's they last time I'm saying that!" They bought me drinks and dinners and all that good stuff. And the thing was that they didn't want anything from me. We were all just having a good time and good times sometimes meant good sex and sometimes it meant "please leave before I wake up."

Like I said, it's those damned dirty thirties. I now knew how teenaged boys feel. It's like you *have* to have it. If you don't get some, you *will* go crazy. Just thinking about it was enough to send me over the edge sometimes. Sex, sex, sex. It's all I had on my mind some days and on those days I couldn't get through the day without getting some. Sometimes I got so horny I could have humped a tree. But I didn't have to hump trees. I could hump real men instead and that's because I developed this great thing called confidence. And once confidence was back on my side, the world was my oyster.

That was about two years ago. In two years, I went from being a fat, frumpy housewife to a sex kitten. I went from a person who was miserable and found happiness in a candy bar to a person who laughed and enjoyed life. And all it took was me getting up off my ass and changing my attitude. All it took was a sight change of circumstance to show me what I was capable of.

It was like my whole world opened up once I took the blinders off and allowed myself to see outside of the box I was living in. I was so glad I didn't let the bad times get to me. I was so glad I waited them out and transformed my life; otherwise I wouldn't have my boys now.

Oh, yeah, getting back to my boys, Zack and Wes. Wes and Zack were like a godsend to me. They gave me anything and everything I wanted and all I had to do was ask. And they both tolerated one another and, though they weren't really friends or anything, they got off on the threesomes as much as I did. It's not a big deal. We only did it occasionally. Well, at least once a week. I have to have it at *least* once a week and the rest of the week was up to them.

Wes once said, "I get Monday and Tuesdays for sure. He can't have you on those days."

Zack agreed and said, "I have to have Friday nights so we can go to a club or two and I can show you off."

So, it worked out fine. They shared me, I shared myself. And we enjoyed our fun.

It's funny, but none of us were that jealous. Of one another, I mean. Sometimes I would see them checking out other women but I didn't mind. Sure, I'd get a little pang of jealousy, but I'd ignore it and just chill until it went away. I didn't have ownership issues. I knew they were independent of me, each of them breathing from a different set of lungs than me. I knew that someday it could end and it could end badly. So, I enjoyed it for what it was and it was good fucking. This ownership thing people have with one another is crazy. I don't get it. However, I do admit that if one of them wanted to bring in another girl, I might have freaked out. Maybe not. But this wasn't about another girl; it was about me being their girl and their slut in the bedroom.

So life was good. Life was so fucking good that I wanted more and more. And then I wanted to share it.

Goodbye, party-time.

Before I met Zack, there was Wes and Wes only. We were an item. We were together. There wasn't talk of threesomes or anything like that. It was just he and I in our own little world. We'd been together every day since the first moment we'd laid eyes on one another. We didn't need anyone else.

We had met in a club and that had been it. Once I saw him, no other guy mattered. It was like, *who is that?* There seemed to be this magnetic force pulling us together. We circled each other for a few minutes before he made a move. I just stood there and waited. And I waited because I knew something phenomenal was about to happen.

"Hello," he said finally.

"Uh," I stammered. "Uh, hello."

"I'm Wes," he said, extending his hand.

"Katrina," I replied and felt more nervous than I had ever felt in my entire life. Who *was* this guy? Where *did* he come from? And *how* could I get him into my bed? But I was almost afraid to touch him. I might get an electric shock. That's how strong the connection was.

He smiled at me, leaned in and whispered in my ear, "Wanna get out of here?"

Wanna get out of here? Hell, yeah, I did. But then, I felt weird. I'd just met this guy. I stared at him, at his handsome face and before I could let bad thoughts of him possibly being a weirdo take over my brain, he smiled at me. In that smile, I saw something. I don't know what it was, but it was like I knew I could trust him. I wanted to trust him. That's what life is sometimes about, isn't it? Trusting someone. I didn't get a bad vibe off of him in the least. It was like I had been waiting on him to show up. And then, there he was.

Before I could change my mind, I nodded and followed him out of the club. Yeah, just like that. I didn't question it. That would have been stupid. I felt really nervous around him but at the same time, at ease. Like I'd been waiting around and wondering when he'd show up and then when he did, I knew. I knew he was *the one.* I don't know how I knew, but I just did.

We didn't say anything as we left the club and got into his car. What could we have said? "Nice to meet you" wasn't in our lingo. It's like we knew we were going to go fuck each other's brains out. And we knew we couldn't do anything about it.

He took me back to his house. It was great place in

the suburbs with a huge entranceway. It was also tastefully and stylishly decorated. I didn't give a shit about the house. I was all about him. I couldn't wait for him to touch me.

He didn't wait long either. As he prepared us a drink, I sat on his couch and sized him up. He was probably the best looking guy I'd ever seen. Tall and handsome. He had a great smile, which he used often. His hands were large and I was willing to bet his dick was too.

He handed me my drink and I threw it back. He chuckled and sat down right next to me. I was so nervous I could have jumped out of my skin and run away. I almost wanted to. But I couldn't. He was going to take me somewhere good. I couldn't wait to go.

"How long have you been in Vegas?" I asked to break the silence.

"Let's talk later," he said and took the glass out of my hand, placed it beside his on the coffee table and then we just jumped at each other. No need for small talk. No need for anything but touching and kissing. And groping.

I moaned as his lips met mine for the first time. They were cool and strong. They pressed against mine until my mouth opened and his tongue came in to play with mine. I moaned again and felt him push me back on the couch. I went willingly and lay down as he settled on top. We were pawing at each other, tugging and ripping at our clothes. He grabbed my shirt and ripped it open and dove in for my breasts which were waiting and *needing* him to play with them. It felt so

28

good when his big hand finally closed over one and squeezed, then his mouth was on my nipple, sucking it into his mouth and playing with it. His tongue stroked it as he sucked and before he pulled back, he gave it a little bite.

"Ahh," I moaned. "Don't stop."

He wasn't about to. He was making a path down my body with his mouth and hands and tongue. No inch was left untouched. I arched away from the couch when his face stopped at my pussy. The anticipation was too much. It was unbearable. To have his face and his lips on my pussy, on that part of me, was like heaven. My skirt was off in one quick motion and his face was pressed between my legs, just pressed and then he breathed me in, breathed my smell in. That made my juices flow even more. I was so turned on by this man.

He took his time to explore my pussy, to explore every single inch of it, like he wanted to know what it was all about. All the while, he was giving me this immense pleasure, this deep, yet light pleasure that just felt right. There was no better feeling in the world than to know he loved being down there, between my legs, sucking at me and licking at me and telling me he loved everything about me, about my body that he'd do something like that to prove it.

The orgasm, the first one of the night, was quick. Before I knew what I was doing, I had grabbed onto his head and was humping his face. He went with me, not letting my pussy or clit away from his mouth or tongue until I was spent. He kept at it until I was nearly howling from the pleasure and then he grabbed onto my ass, scooped me up and gave me one final lick, a long one right down my slit.

I was so turned on I could have came again from that.

Before I had a chance to do it, he was on me, in me, pushing his big, hard cock right up in me, not letting me move one single inch as he gained control of me. And he was in control. I loved that. He could have it. He did a good job with it and we both knew that where fucking was concerned, there could only be one chief. And it was him. He was fucking me, fucking my brains out. My senses were all on fire and I just wanted him, all of him, on me and at me and touching me and groping me and kissing me all at once.

"You're so tight," he moaned into my ear and licked it. "Such a tight pussy."

"Your cock is so big," I moaned back and sucked on his neck, then gritted my teeth because it felt so good. "God, I love your cock!"

"I love your pussy," he said and fucked me harder. "I'm gonna fuck it."

"Oh, fuck it, baby," I moaned and suddenly felt the orgasm. "Don't stop! Please, don't stop!"

He didn't stop. He couldn't have stopped if he wanted to. He fucked me so hard and for so long, my legs were trembling. It's like they had turned to jelly. I fucked back, squeezing his hard cock into my pussy for everything it was worth. I loved fucking him as much as I loved getting fucked by him, with his hard cock. We were both coming at the same time and the couch was shaking, the window panes were shaking and then the eruption and then the peace after it filtered away.

Afterwards, we couldn't do anything but lie there and pant. After the panting subsided, the kissing started again and then the touching and before I knew what was happening, he had me up on all fours and was fucking me doggie style and I was taking every single inch of his hard cock.

This went on half the night and we fell asleep in each other's arms. And we've been together ever since.

Just let me stop here and say that Wes had the most beautiful fuck face in the world. I loved his fuck face and I was beginning to love him. He was so good. He was one of those guys girls dream about when they dream about their dream guys, *that's* how good he was. He gave me flowers and backrubs and gifts to show his appreciation and devotion. He bought me a trip to a spa because he said I was working too hard and needed a break. He cooked dinner for me on a weekly basis. He called if he was going to be late or couldn't make it for a date. He took me out, he kept me in, and every night that we were together, he fucked me good.

He was getting ready to do just that now. I was the happiest woman in the world.

He began to undress me, taking his time. I loved that he did that, that he took care with me, that he rubbed my bare skin before bending down to kiss it. He paused. I wondered if something was wrong.

"I love you," he said out of nowhere.

I jerked myself out of good-feeling land and stared at him, mouth agape. "What did you just say?"

He smiled and kissed his way back up my body. "I said I love you, I love you, I love you."

I was dumbstruck.

"I mean it," he said before kissing me on the lips. "I love you."

I felt all… I dunno, butterfly-ie. It was a wonderful feeling, don't get me wrong, but did this mean my party days were over? Was my good-times lifestyle gone? Had my party-time ended? We'd only been seeing each other for a few months and hell, I just got divorced. This was all…all of a sudden. It scared the shit out of me.

He stopped kissing me and swallowed hard. He was waiting. He was waiting for confirmation. He had put himself out there and now he wondered if he was going to get burned.

I didn't know what the fuck to do.

I looked into his eyes and felt… So good to have him staring back at me. So what if my party-time was over? Big deal. So what if I'd only had a good year to get my groove on with a few other men? I didn't have good, intense orgasms with them. But I did have Wes and he was worth a thousand men, or in my case, five or six. Maybe seven. And he was so good. He was kind and sweet and cute and had a great set of arms and he had a great job and knew a lot of groovy people. He drove a Jaguar and made me breakfast in bed and… Well, you can see why I didn't want to let him get away. Any man that brings a girl breakfast in bed is a keeper. Especially if he prepared eggs the way Wes did. He always sprinkled a little shredded cheese on top.

"I love you, too," I said and felt it, really felt that love inside of me for him. I was ready to move on. Tony had moved on. He and I had kept in contact and had actually become really good friends. But he had his permanent sweet thing so it was only fair that I should have mine.

A look of relief swept over Wes's face and he grinned. I grinned back and opened my arms to him. He fell into me and hugged me tight. I sighed with happiness. How fucking good life was. How fucking good.

"Phew," he said and kissed my neck. "I was beginning to wonder."

"Sorry, I kept you waiting," I said and licked his ear a little.

He pulled back and said, "You mean it, don't you?"

"Of course, I mean it," I said and felt a little shock that he would think I *didn't*.

"Sure?"

"Yes, I'm sure," I said and almost giggled. "God, you're so serious right now!"

"Sorry," he muttered. "You had me worried for a minute."

I wrapped my arms around his neck and said, "You're not worried anymore, are you?"

He shook his head happily.

"Good," I said and pushed my face towards his for a kiss.

"Mmm," he moaned and kissed me. "I think we should get married."

I froze. He stopped kissing me and pulled back just as my eyes nearly popped out of my head. He couldn't be serious. No way. He held one finger up for me to wait, got out of the bed, raced out of the room and came back with a ring box.

He was serious.

"Will you marry me?" he asked and opened the box.

I stared at the ring. It was gorgeous. It was platinum and diamond. I stared at him. "Are you serious?"

He nodded.

I stared back at the ring, then back at him and then, it all made sense. Even though I'd already been married once and it ended badly, even though it made me nervous to think about doing it again, even though I liked being single, it all made perfect sense. Maybe because he was the one asking.

"Yes," I said.

"Really?" he asked, grinning.

"Yes!" I squealed and threw my arms around his neck and began to kiss his face. "Yes, yes, yes!"

"Then let's do it."

I grinned at him. This was too perfect. And it was a little too easy. There *had* to be a catch. I batted my eyes a little and muttered, "You really wanna marry me?"

"Yes, Katrina," he said. "I do."

Huh. So, goodbye, party-time. Hello... I stopped and thought. Oh, hell. Hello, marriage. Again.

"Uh, Wes?" I said.

"Yeah?" he asked and moved in closer to me.

I breathed in his smell, loved it. It made me horny, his smell. He always smelled so good. Oh, forget it. Forget about asking stupid questions. Forget about ruining the moment. Forget about everything but this.

"What is it?" he asked and pulled back.

"Oh, nothing," I said and wrapped my arms around his neck and pulled him close to me. "Let's fuck."

So we did.

The catch.

We didn't set a date or anything like that. We didn't move in together. He kept his house and I kept mine and our schedules remained the same. Sometimes, he'd sleep over at my house and sometimes I'd sleep over at his. Sometimes, we'd go a day or two without seeing each other. This was great because once we hooked up again, the sex was out of this world. Being skin-starved for a few days always makes the sex so much better.

I kept my own life and he kept his. We met in the middle of it all. Nothing much changed besides the fact that I wore an engagement ring. It's like we just decided to get married and then decided not to do much about it. Sure we talked about it from time to time and I even tried on a few wedding gowns. Well, I bought one but I hid it in the closet. I know it was stupid but the dress was perfect. My first wedding consisted of a plain white dress and a cake in a church reception room. I wanted this one to be better. So I bought the dress because not only was it perfect but I knew if I waited, it would be gone. Or just in case Wes wanted to run down to the Little Chapel one day. I wanted to be prepared. I knew the pictures in that dress would be phenomenal. I imagined plastering them all over my house.

But as time went by, I began to notice that something was off. Wes began to act a little differently towards me. He didn't withdraw or anything like that, he just stopped talking about getting married. I didn't let it bother me. I was in no rush to get married again. But if I did get married, I wanted to marry him. Still, it was puzzling.

"Katrina, I have something to tell you," he said over dinner one night.

I nodded and looked around the crowded restaurant, then back at him. "Okay, honey."

He gave me a tight smile and said in a rush, "I love you, I think you know that. You're fantastic and everything I've ever wanted in a girl, in a woman. You're smart, beautiful, bold and vivacious."

Vivacious? Well, if you say so. I couldn't help but grin like a fool. I was vivacious! Me!

"I love that about you," he said and took a breath. "In fact, I love everything about you. It's not that."

I nodded, smiling at him. *Keep talking baby, this is all good.*

"I love that we get along so well," he said. "We don't fight like other people, you know? And we don't

36

crowd each other, either."

He was so getting a blowjob tonight.

"It's not that I have a problem with our relationship or anything," he said. "It's not that at all. It's just… It's just I have this one problem."

I sighed, not really listening to what he was saying anymore. Flattery always made my short attention span kick in.

He kept on even though I wasn't paying attention, "But there's one problem. I don't want to spend the rest of my life not ever sleeping with another woman. I have to have that."

He finished and gave me a shy smile, as if to seek my approval. I smiled back. "You think I'm vivacious?"

The smile slid off his face and he said, "Uh…yeah, I guess…"

I grinned. "Wow."

"So?" he asked.

I shook myself. I was still hung up on the "vivacious" part and all the other stuff. He thought I was vivacious! Vivacious. That's a good word. All that other stuff he'd said was good, too but vivacious was great.

"Katrina?" he asked.

I sighed happily, still lost in my thoughts. I'd finally found him. Mr. Right. There he was, sitting right in front of me. Tall. Dark. Devastatingly handsome. He said nice things about me. We were going to get married! I was going to look so good in that dress.

He cleared his throat and seemed a little agitated.

"Katrina, did you hear me?"

No. I hadn't. I was in La La Land. I liked being in La La Land. He gave me a little glare and crossed his arms. What was wrong with him?

I sat up and said, "What'd you say, honey? I'm sorry, I didn't hear you."

He didn't allow his agitation to take over. He stared me dead in the eye and said, "If we get married, I plan to continue sleeping with other women."

Of course I had been taking a sip of wine and as soon as the words were out of his mouth, I choked. After I got my breath back, I shook my head at him and muttered, "Wha...?"

"You heard me," he said. "Didn't you?"

"I don't..." I began. "I mean... Did you just tell me that you want to sleep with other women?"

He nodded, and then quickly said, "Not now. I'm talking about in the future."

In the future? Wait a minute. Was he...? Did he...? I sat there for a moment, confused, then I got it. What the fuck?! Now I was good enough but soon he'd tire of me. That's what he meant. What a bastard! What the hell was going on here?! What happened to my happy world? How could he do this? I was having so much fun with all this relationship bliss I must have gone dumb. Suddenly, I was angry. I was good and pissed off. I knew it! I knew there was a catch! *This* was the catch! He wasn't perfect and he never would be! He was just like Tony, just like every other man out there!

Wait a minute. Maybe I had read it all wrong. Oh, hell, I knew I hadn't. And why had he told me this here? In our restaurant? The one he always took me took to on "special" occasions. Was this a special occasion? No, he'd said it here because he didn't want me to freak out. We were in public and that meant I'd have to behave like a good little girl. *The bastard!* Who did he think he was dealing with here? An imbecile? A stupid girl? Oh, he had another thing coming.

But…maybe I had read him wrong.

"What exactly do you mean?" I asked innocently.

He glanced around the restaurant, nodded at someone he knew, and then looked back at me.

"Well?" I asked, getting slightly agitated at him.

"It's like this," he said and lowered his voice. "I can't settle down. I mean, I can. I can give you everything you want. I can give you that white picket fence, I can give you kids, money to shop or do whatever you want to with. But I can't give you *every*thing."

"Really?" I said and thought about why I had agreed to marry him. Hell, I was having a good time being single, too! But I didn't want to fuck any other man besides him. He was perfect. He was a good lover. And that's why I'd agreed. He was fucking perfect! I wasn't about to let him go. I'd put too much work into him, into this relationship. I'd read all the fucking books, done the research. I was a good, if not great, lover. At least above average. I gave head on a consistent basis. In fact, I liked to give head. I especially liked to give it to him. Now I didn't want to.

"Katrina, I just want to be honest with you," he said and grabbed my hands. "I can't give you my loyalty. I can't be faithful to only one woman. I've tried. I've been married once before, you know that. It didn't work out because I cheated. And I cheated because it's in me to cheat."

And because all the women in the world were throwing themselves at him. The bitches.

"But what *are* you saying?" I asked, near tears. "You don't want to get married?"

Oh, God! I'd paid a fortune for that wedding dress! I'd had it altered, too. I couldn't get a refund. I was so stupid.

He sighed as though he was trying to come to terms with himself. And with me. He finally said, "I want to marry you."

"So do it."

"I won't do it unless you agree."

"Agree to what?" I asked, exasperated.

"To allowing me my freedom."

That stung. *I want you as long as I can fuck around on you.* Oh, shit, shit, *SHIT!* It was true, wasn't it? Men were all bastards. They were all dogs. They were all hell-bent on ruining the lives of all women!

"Listen," I said slowly. "If you want to break up with me, you can come out and say it."

"I don't want to break up with you."

"Then what the fuck do you want?" I hissed and several people glanced over at us. Oh, fuck them anyway.

"Shh," he said. "Keep your voice down."

"I won't keep my voice down," I hissed. "I've spent a fortune on a fucking dress that I'm not going to get to wear!"

"I'll pay for it."

"Ah ha!" I snapped. "You do want out."

He was letting the agitation seep through just a little bit. "No, I don't want out. I want to marry you. I love you."

"But I'm not enough," I snapped. "Is that it?"

He shook his head. "Yes. No! You're turning it all around on me! I don't know! I mean, you're enough right now. You're everything to me. Right now. But it all changes, honey."

"We can be different!"

"No, we can't," he said. "I thought the same thing with my ex-wife—"

"Please stop bringing her up!" I hissed. "I don't talk to you about Tony!"

"I'm trying to make a point."

"So make it. You're beginning to piss me off," I said, though I was hanging on his every word, on every syllable. What if he was my last chance at a good man? Good men were so damned hard to find and if you were lucky enough to find one there was always, always a catch. They had twelve kids from previous relationships or were just plain crazy. I was thirty-two. If I didn't get married soon, I'd be one of those pathetic women out there who had pictures of their cats in their offices instead of their kids. Cause they didn't have any kids! They had cats! I was terrified of being a "Cat Lady".

"Do you love me?" he asked.

That threw me. My mouth fell open but I managed to say, "Of *course* I love you."

The waiter was nearing our table with our food. We spotted him at the same time. I pulled back from the table just as he put the plates in front of us.

"Fresh ground peppercorn?" he asked and produced a big brown pepper grinder thing from thin air.

"No, thanks," I said and suddenly couldn't take it anymore. The walls were closing in on me and I was having trouble breathing. I suddenly wanted to run from the restaurant and disappear.

He held the thing out to Wes, who shook his head. He asked, "Is there anything else I can get you?"

"The check," I said and pushed my plate away.

"Is there something—?"

"No," I said and threw my napkin on the table dramatically before I hurried out. "Nothing's wrong."

"Of fuck," I heard Wes mutter as I made my way out.

My ex-husband, Tony, and I were really good friends. How weird was that? A few years ago we were ready to kill each other over our divorce but after a while, we because best friends. We shared everything. Well, most everything. We didn't have sex anymore.

As soon as I got home, I picked up the phone and spilled my guts to him. He listened, contemplated, sighed, coughed and gave pause. When I was done, I wiped the tears from my eyes.

"Marry him," he said.

"You're only saying that cause you're sick of paying me alimony!" I snapped.

"Yeah," he said slowly. "But he seems like a nice guy."

"You did too, asshole." I lit a cigarette and smoked as I said, "I'm going to call it off."

"No, you can't do that."

"What can I do, then?" I asked.

"Marry him," he said. "And stop complaining."

"Oh, you men are all the same," I said. "I bet you wanted something like that."

He didn't respond.

"Tony?"

"Well, I thought about bringing it up but, but then…"

"What?" I asked.

"I didn't think you would go for it."

"Why?"

"I just didn't."

I rolled my eyes before responding, "Whatever."

"Look at it this way," he said. "He's a man and at least he's willing to admit he's a man. He's being honest about it."

I was stumped.

"You know?" he said.

"But, Tony," I said, about to start crying again. "He said he won't be faithful to me!"

"No one can ever be faithful to another person," he said.

"Especially in *your* case," I couldn't help but say, but then felt bad about saying it. "Sorry, I didn't mean it like that."

"Then how do you mean it?" he asked and sighed.

"I just didn't mean to be a bitch."

"Listen, Katrina, people screw around, we both know that firsthand," he said. "Life isn't like the movies. We're human and humans like to fuck."

"What the hell are you talking about? You haven't turned into a swinger, have you?"

"Nooo," he said slowly. "Think about it. An affair broke us up. Maybe we didn't have to break up."

"But you fell in love with her!" I snapped.

"But I still loved you!" he snapped back. "I told you that but you told me to leave."

He's right. I had. But then I told him he could stay. He left anyway.

"I'm talking about you facing up to reality," he said more calmly. "You've got a good guy and you're gonna kick his ass out, just like you did mine, so you can—"

"I didn't kick you out, ass," I said. "You left."

"Well, if I had stayed, you wouldn't have made it easy on me."

"Why should I have made it easy on you?"

"I don't know," he said. "And then you go and get beautiful and then..."

"Oh, shit," I muttered. "Tony, shut up."

"Well, why didn't you lose that weight when we were together?"

"You're awful!" I exclaimed. "Anyway. What about my situation?"

"Marry him," he said. "You do love him, right?"

"Yeah," I said. "But what does that have to do with anything? He'll still cheat on me."

"He's gonna do it anyway," he said. "And then you

can kick his ass out. And for what? Cause he admits to liking pussy? Newsflash—men like pussy."

"*Tony!*"

"Well," he said. "It's true. Men love pussy."

Sometimes I wished we hadn't remained friends.

"You let him go, Katrina," he said. "And I can guarantee you of one thing."

"Of what?"

"Of being alone."

I froze. He was right. Sure, I'd get another guy, then what? Maybe fall in love with him? Maybe not. I'd settle. If I let Wes go, I'd have to settle on some guy who couldn't match his socks, who listened to top forty radio *all the time*, who forgot to shave on weekends, who would never, ever be as good as Wes was. Cause Wes I loved. I loved him so much. Not just his looks or money—though those were fine attributes—but loved the way he talked and smoked and fucked and... OH SHIT!

"This isn't helping me!" I yelled.

"Well, it should. You need to stop being so stubborn."

"I will not marry a man that will cheat on me."

"Then you aren't never gonna marry again," he said. "And if you do get one that doesn't cheat, don't think he isn't thinking about it."

I scowled at the phone for a good minute. I could tell he was scowling back. I hung up. Fuck him anyway. I stared at the phone and grabbed it, dialing his number.

He picked up, and knowing it was me, said, "Think

45

about it like this. What if it were your idea?"

"My idea?"

"What if you were the one who brought it up?" he asked. "You told me yourself that you didn't necessarily want to be married again. Think of it like that. You get married and you can still have fun."

"I don't know…" I sighed. "Everything's fine as it is. Why should either of us screw with it?"

"*Because* people get bored, just like we got bored," he said. "That's the way it goes. At least you both know upfront what you're dealing with."

There really was no going back. There really was no knight in shining armor. No perfect man. They didn't exist. Wes did admit it to me, so if it happened, *if* he cheated in the future, it's not like I hadn't been warned. Why was life so fucking complicated?

"Well, I gotta go, Tony," I said.

"Just think about it," he said. "He seems like a good guy."

And that was the whole problem.

Caved.

So, I caved. Though I really didn't feel like doing it, I figured I could do something about the cheating situation later on. I told Wes I had reconsidered and I would agree and then we made up. But I felt uneasy about the whole thing. I just didn't want to share him. I wanted him all to myself. I deserved him!

"What do you think about us getting another girl?"

Wes asked later that week.

I screeched, "WES!"

He recoiled as if I'd slapped him. "Just kidding. Why are you so edgy?"

"Because," I said slowly. "You told me you couldn't be faithful to me and it's still freaking me out a little."

He nodded. "Did you want me to lie?"

"Yes!"

He sighed. "Is this really bothering you that much?"

I nodded. "Yeah, it is. And I don't want it to. I mean, I'm not a kid anymore and once you're married things change. I mean, I was married before."

He nodded. "Maybe it's just too soon."

"Too soon?"

"Us getting married," he said. "Maybe we should wait."

Great. I knew it was too good to be true. He'd want to "wait" and to "postpone" and then he'd leave me a fucking note on the kitchen counter one morning: *"Dear Katrina, It's over. Bye. Wes."*

"I don't want to wait," I muttered. "I mean, it's complicated and I just don't think it should be this hard."

He took my hand. "I think *you* need to wait, baby, not me. I know what I want and I want you but I don't want this to eat you up inside."

"It isn't eating me up inside!"

He eyed me before responding, "Yeah, it is. Jealousy can do that."

"I'm not jealous!" I yelled. "Why are you saying

47

that?"

"You're not jealous now," he said. "Because I'm not doing anything but what if I came home one day and told you I had hooked up with someone else?"

The thought made me nauseous. It really did. But was it my problem it made me sick to my stomach? Yeah, it was. I was more afraid of how I would react than I was afraid of his actual doing it. I was afraid I couldn't handle it and would sink into a deep depression after I found out. I was just, simply, afraid.

"See?" he said when I didn't respond.

"See what?" I said and felt tears stream down my cheeks. "I just want us to be together."

"And that's all I want, too," he said.

"I'm just afraid it will all change, Wes," I said.

He nodded. "The thing is, baby, that fear is just holding you back. Well, it's holding both of us back. I want to be with a woman I can share everything with. I thought you were that woman. When we met, I thought, *she's perfect!* I could see us together for years and years. I felt so comfortable with you that I thought I could bring up the fidelity issue."

Boy, that made me feel like crap. It's like he had this image of me being this free spirit and I'd crushed it. He thought I was more open than I actually was.

"Were you disappointed in me?" I asked quietly.

"A little," he said. "But if that's the way it goes, then that's the way it goes. I mean, I want to be with you. I can give you almost everything but you can't have it all. I want something for myself. Otherwise, we'd both go crazy, baby."

48

I swallowed hard. He was right. Why make an issue of it? More importantly, why deny it? We were built this way, we weren't built for monogamy. If we were, Tony and I would still be together, happy in our ignorance of all the other things—and people—out there.

"Am I not good enough?" I cried and felt it, felt so low and undesirable and just bad. This was killing me and it hadn't even happened yet. Love was so close to pain. There were on the same level, love and pain. One moment, happiness, another moment, pure dread and misery. It was almost enough to make a person not want to mess with any of it. I stared at him. He was worth it. I knew that. But how could I get through this without hurting both of us? I should just be happy he'd been so honest with me. But I wasn't.

"Of course you are," he said. "You're better than good."

"You don't really think that."

"I do," he said and pulled me into his lap. "I really do. Listen, let's forget about it. Let's take it slow. Let's wait a year so we'll grow and we'll know for sure. I shouldn't have rushed you."

But I had wanted to be rushed and swept off my feet. I just didn't want Mr. Honesty ruining my fairy tale. But was it better that he had told me before or if he'd just cheated? I didn't know but I did know I wished he'd just kept his big mouth shut.

"Is that okay?" he asked and kissed my cheek. "Wait a year and see?"

I nodded.

He grinned at me and pulled my face to his and we kissed. And then it didn't seem to matter. Maybe I could change him. That wasn't going to happen. Leopards don't change their spots. Maybe *I* could change. But I knew that probably wasn't going to happen, either.

Cat and mouse.

The year seemed to fly by and before long, I was caught up again in that magical feeling of love and hope and all that crap. I was so happy that when this happened, I was jolted back to reality.

It was a nice reality, don't get me wrong. Just totally unexpected.

"Hi," he said. "I heard you were the best."

I just stared at him, at this stranger. At this man. *Who was he?*

"I mean, best trainer," he said and seemed to blush. "*Trainer.*"

I kept staring at him. Who was this guy? And where did he come from? It was like he was perfect. Nothing was wrong with him. Had a factory assembled him? If so, I wanted to buy stock in it.

And he wanted me to train him? He was already in great shape and those arms, oh, my God! I hadn't seen a set of arms like that in years. Wes had great arms, but this guy's were bigger and stronger and... Oh. Me. God.

"So do you think you can help me?" he asked.

I started to say something, but then realized I had

merely squeaked instead of answering him. I cleared my throat and managed to get out, "What's your name?"

"Zack."

"Oh," I said and smiled up at him. He was *so* tall. "I'm Katrina."

"I know your name," he said and leaned in towards me. "They told me you were the best."

"They?"

"The people at the front counter."

I stared past all the fitness equipment and in the general direction of the front counter of the gym. "They" must have been Nick and Helen. They worked the front counter and trained part-time. Sometimes all three of us went out and got shit-faced. Since I'd been seeing Wes, we didn't do it that much.

He nodded. "So can you help me?"

I stared at him. He had big, brown beautiful eyes and a masculine jaw line and just looked good enough to eat. He was tall. He was well built and...I was getting married. I was in love with Wes. *Hello!?*

"So," I said, slipping into business mode. "What is it you want?"

He stared at me and I felt his eyes. Like what he wanted was me. I shook myself. No. He didn't want me. He probably had to beat the women off. But so did Wes.

Wes. Good. Yes, think about Wes. Wes who was going to marry me. *Some*day. Wes who respected me and loved me and never mentioned the cheating thing again after our talk about it. Now the cheating thing didn't seem like such a big deal. If he got to cheat, would I get to cheat, too? And could I start with Zack?

"I just want to work on my cardio," he said. "I heard you do running hikes."

I nodded. "Yeah, sometimes at Valley of the Fire. It's really hard. Not that you couldn't do it or anything...I mean, you look healthy and... Yeah."

"That's what I want."

"Okay," I said. "But I have to tell you, we have to meet very early and—"

"I don't have a problem with that," he said.

"Oh? Oh. Good."

"So can we do it?" he asked.

"Sure," I said, nodding. "I'm not sure when I can do it, but I can schedule you in. I'll have to get back with you, though. I'm kinda busy right now."

"That's cool," he said, then pulled out his wallet and handed me a business card. "There's my number."

I took it and looked it over. Zack Parson was his name. Parsons? Where had I heard that name before? Parsons... A lightbulb went off in my head. Oh, he was a *Parsons*. He was from the Parsons family and they owned a bunch of casinos! He was filthy stinking rich. Wes was well off but he wasn't rich like this guy and—

I was going to marry Wes because he and I loved one another and this guy was probably gay anyway. Look at him. He dressed well even for the gym. Of course, he wasn't training today and his outfit of a nice button-down cotton shirt and jeans and leather shoes were... Nice. He looked damn good. Damn it. Why did I have to already be in love with someone else?

"Cool," I said, not knowing what else to say. "Let me check my schedule and I'll get back with you."

He nodded and headed towards the door, then stopped, turned and said, "It was very nice to meet you, Katrina."

So formal. I couldn't help but grin at him. He was trying to impress me. I liked that. I liked being impressed. I liked that he was the one doing it.

"You, too, Zack."

"So," he said and smiled shyly. "Just give me a call, okay?"

"Will do," I said and watched him leave the building.

I took Zack to the Valley of the Fire the following Thursday morning. I was usually off on Thursdays but I made an exception for him. Not because he was Zack Parsons or because he was cute or anything like that. I did it because I could use the extra money. My old dishwasher was on its last legs and I wanted a new one. Preferably one that didn't sound like a rocket launcher whenever I turned it on. I could have bought one on credit, of course, but I'd finally paid my debt off and was hesitant to get back in. From now on, I wanted to pay cash for everything, if at all possible. So, it had nothing to do with Zack. At least that's what I told myself.

We met at the gym around five in the morning and he insisted on driving his SUV. I climbed into it and felt a little uncomfortable. What if he kidnapped me? What if he did something gross and I wanted to get away from him but couldn't? What if he left me in the desert with no food or water?

But the real question was *what if he makes a pass at me?*

And that made me nervous. What if he made a pass at me? I would remain strong. I wasn't a cheater. I had been cheated on and it was a bad, bad thing. Besides that, I was a professional. I never dated my clients. Never.

However, none of my clients were as cute as him.

We made it to the Valley of the Fire in about an hour. The place was breathtaking. Lots of big, red rocks and open desert terrain. A few rabbits and a few cactuses. Or cacti. Lots of space that was one-hundred percent deserted at this early hour. It was a little chilly out as well. I almost wished I hadn't agreed to this.

I shook myself and we got out of the SUV and told him, "Let's start with a little warm-up."

"Okay," he said and grinned.

I demonstrated a few leg and groin stretch and then we did a few sprints. After that, I said, "Now take it slow at first because you don't want to overexert yourself all at once. We're going to go up and around the rocks, mostly running on the sand. This is really good for your calves."

He leaned back and checked out my calves. "Do you do this a lot?"

"Sometimes," I said.

"Your calves are great," he said and got another look at them.

"I hate them," I said.

"But they're so shapely and muscular."

"Yeah, but when I try on a pair of knee-high boots, I can't zip them up over them."

He smiled. "You should never cover those things up."

I blushed. Why he was making such a big deal over my calves? I knew they were nice but all the same I almost wished he'd shut up.

"Anyway," I said. "You ready?"

He was still staring at me.

I stared at him. "What is it?"

"You have such a tight little body," he said and stood back from me. "I mean... Wow! Look at you... Wow."

"Well, that's what I get paid to do," I said. "You ready?"

He nodded and we began to jog. He kept sprinting ahead of me and then would jog in place until I caught up. It was annoying as hell. I was the trainer, okay? Just because your legs are longer than mine doesn't mean I'm not in charge. We did this for about twenty minutes. Then I told him to slow down and walk for a while, then we'd speed up.

"Sounds good," he said and started sprinting off again.

I let him go and decided he really didn't want to train. He wanted to play. I let him get ahead one more time and when he stopped to wait, I sped up and flew past him. He immediately took off after me. Of course, he caught up in no time. I turned around to look at him. He held out his hands like he was a monster after me and I started laughing. He was laughing, too. We were like two little kids playing hide and seek. Except neither one of was hiding.

But I couldn't help but think, *let me get this straight, this guy wants to work out but all he does is act stupid. Why?*

I knew why. I knew exactly why. I also knew the game wasn't hide and seek. It was cat and mouse.

I picked up my speed and managed to get ahead, though I was still laughing. I was laughing so hard I didn't even feel myself trip over the rock. All I knew was that there was an incredible amount of sand in my face and my knee was throbbing.

Oh, fucking shit.

"Are you okay?" Zack said and rolled me over.

"Ow!" I screamed as pain shot up through my leg. I didn't want to look down at it. I didn't want to see how bad it was. I peeked. Oh, God. My knee was red and swollen and that meant I would be out of commission for at least a couple of days. *Great.*

"Does it hurt?" he asked.

"Yeah, you could say that," I said sarcastically.

"Do you need to go to the hospital?"

"No," I said. "I'll be okay. I just need to pack it in some ice and take a few aspirin."

"We can do that."

I almost smiled gratefully at him but winced instead as another pain shot up through my leg.

"Here," he said and in one fell swoop, picked me up. "Let's get you back to the truck."

I pushed against his chest and said, "No, it's okay. I can walk."

"Like hell you can," he said and carried me all the way to his SUV. And it was a good distance, too—almost a mile. He carried me the whole way, never stopping to rest. He carried me like I weighed only a pound. I never felt so girly before in my life than I did up in his big, strong arms.

He put me in the back seat, told me to stretch out and then he drove like a bat out of hell until we got to a convenience store where he went in and purchased some ice for my knee and a bottle of water so I could pop a few aspirin.

I watched in amazement as he pulled his t-shirt off and ripped it apart, then packed ice into it and placed it on my throbbing knee. I sat up and held it over my knee and he pulled back, leaning in the frame of the door. All of a sudden, I really noticed his body and almost became mesmerized by it. His body was fantastic. It was hot. His chest was tanned and wide and tight, so masculine. His pecs were defined to perfection. I glanced at his shoulders and arms which were just as perfect as his chest. I imagined being snuggled up in his arms; they were so big and strong. My eyes went lower to his stomach. He had a six-pack. For a brief moment I imagined my hands sliding down his chest to his stomach and then to his—

What the fuck was wrong with me?! My knee throbbed again and I groaned with pain. Good. Pain takes away the bad thoughts.

He grinned and opened my water, handed it to me

and said, "Anything else?"

Yeah, just lean in here for a minute and let me touch your big arms. Just for a moment. I'll be quick. I shook myself and said, "Actually, I'm dying for a cigarette."

"You smoke?"

I nodded. "Yeah, but don't tell anyone. Trainers and smoking aren't exactly supposed to mix."

"I smoke too," he said and grinned like we had this great thing in common. *Let's be unhealthy together! Yay!*

"Light us up one, then," I said.

He dug into his glove compartment and pulled out a pack, lit us one and as I smoked, he got back into the driver's seat and drove back to Vegas, a little slower than I would have liked. I knew I wasn't in that much pain, but he was driving like grandpa.

As he drove, he chitchatted, telling me all kinds of things about himself. I nodded and occasionally winced in pain from my knee. I once started to ask him to speed up but then realized why he was taking it slow. He was taking it slow so he could prolong the trip. It made me a little uneasy, but not enough to call him on it. I liked listening to him talk.

"Want me to drop you off at your house?" he asked.

"No, just take me to my car," I said. "I can drive."

"I'll drop you off," he said. "Then I can get someone to run by and get your car."

"Zack," I said. "I'm okay. Just take me to the gym."

"I'll take you to your house," he said.

I groaned and gave him the address and in no time

he was pulling up in front of my little stucco house. I always smiled whenever I saw my little house, mainly because it was mine. I took so much pride in it. Once Zack carried me inside, he looked around and told me how nice he thought it was. I grinned. I loved compliments on my house.

"Thanks," I said. "You can put me on the couch."

He lay me down gently and asked me where the blankets were. I told him and he came back with the comforter from the bed and my pillow. He propped me up and then handed me the remote control and then went for another aspirin, some alcohol to clean the scrapes and some bandages. I watched in amazement as he cleaned my knee, bandaged it and handed me an aspirin.

After I took it, I said, "You don't have to make a fuss over me."

"No," he said and sat down in a chair. "I want to."

I smiled and said, "I know you must be busy."

"Actually, no," he said. "I'm free today."

I nodded. Was he planning on hanging around with me all day? He still had his shirt off. He still looked *so* good. I shook myself and said, "I have to say, you're very good at this."

"At what?"

"Taking care of me," I said.

He shrugged. "I like to help people."

"Well, you know what you're doing."

"Thanks," he said, grinning. "Why don't I order us a pizza or something?"

I checked the clock on the wall. It was almost

noon! My stomach grumbled almost on cue and I nodded. He ordered the pizza and tried to get comfortable in my ultra-modern but very uncomfortable chair. I loved that chair. It looked good but no one ever sat in it, not even me.

"You can sit over here," I said and scooted up on the couch. "That way we can both watch TV."

He grinned and came over to the couch. He settled in and I flipped the channels until I came to my favorite talk-show.

"I like this one, too," he said.

I stared at him for a second, then back at the TV. "Don't you have a job?"

"Oh, yeah, I work for a casino," he said. "I'm just taking a leave of absence for a few months."

"Nice life," I muttered.

"It is," he said and grinned.

I shook my head at him and we watched as a transvestite came between lovers.

"Is your knee okay?" he asked.

I nodded. "It feels a lot better."

"Good." He stared at the TV and then back at me. "You want me to rub it?"

All of a sudden, I knew *why* he was hanging around. Oh, yes! OH NO! No, no, no! I had an urge to slap my wrist in shame. But I knew I'd have to set him straight. Even if I didn't want to. I stared at his bodacious body. Why did I have to have a boyfriend? It was so unfair!

"Zack," I said. "You know I have a boyfriend, right?"

His head dropped then he looked back up at me. "I kinda figured a girl like you wasn't on the market."

"A girl like me?"

"Yeah, like you," he said. "Listen, that's okay. I just want to be...friends."

I almost cracked up but I caught myself just in time. "Okay, we can do that. But really, if you have something to do, I can take care of myself."

"No, I don't mind," he said. "And I'm not trying to...you know. I just thought if you wanted me to rub your knee, it might help."

"Well, if you want to."

He nodded eagerly. "I'd love to."

And I'd love you to, I thought.

He pulled the comforter off and lifted my legs, slid under them and rested them gently his lap. He began to rub my knee ever so gently and I lay back and relaxed, really loving the feeling of being pampered, the feeling of him easing the pain with his big hands. I must have dozed off because the next thing I knew, he was rubbing both of my legs, using long strokes. His hands were threatening to get closer and closer to my shorts. I started to sit up and push him away but then I thought why not see what he was going to do. Yeah. Why not?

I knew what he was going to do. I had fantasized about it since the day we met. I wanted it and I wanted it bad. And if meant I was a bad person, then that's what it meant.

His strokes were lighter now as he neared the leg of my shorts. And then he just lifted them with the tip of his finger and began to rub under the fabric. I shuddered with delight, with anticipation. The finger was making its way to my pussy slowly, so slowly I was about to come from the buildup. And then it was on my pussy, sliding between the lips and resting on my clit.

I moaned.

He moved and leaned over me and our lips brushed. We moaned in sync as our mouths opened at the same time and his tongue slipped into my mouth as his hand stayed there, on my pussy.

I moaned and he began to move his finger a little and I found my hips moving too, moving rhythmically to the movement of his finger, to the beat of my heart and before I knew what was happening, I was coming. As I came, a little wail escaped my lips.

That must have been his cue. He got down between my legs, slipped my shorts off gently as not to hurt my knee and dove in. His mouth clamped onto my pussy and he sucked at me until I came again and this time it was a little more vicious, as if the orgasm didn't want to come out and I had to make it. I screamed as I came because it hurt a little to let it go.

And then he was on top of me, his mouth on mine, me smelling myself, tasting myself, tasting my pussy on his mouth. We ate at each other's mouths and I began to stroke his hard cock through his pants. He was about to come out of them when the doorbell rang. We jerked and stared at each other.

"I'll get it," he said.

"No!" I exclaimed. "It might be someone! Get off me! Quick!"

He pulled back and I jumped up, howled in pain

and hopped around. He tried to make me sit but I pushed him down on the couch and threw the comforter over him to hide him and hobbled to the door. I peered through the peephole to see the pizza delivery guy.

Thank you, God!

"Hold on!" I called and grabbed a twenty and a five out of my purse, opened the door a crack and slipped it though. He took it, slid the pizza sideways through the crack and thanked me before he discreetly left.

"Time to eat," I said and turned around.

Zack threw the comforter off, jumped up and ran at me. I just stood there and waited. He grabbed me up in his arms and our lips locked. I dropped the pizza. He carried me all the way to the bedroom where he threw me down on the bed and began to eat at my body, at all of it, not missing one single inch. I just lay there and panted and began to want him until I thought I couldn't stand it another moment, couldn't stand it until he was inside me, fucking me.

He pushed my legs open with his knee, bent over, sucked my nipple in his mouth and as he nibbled at it, he pushed his hard cock into my tight and wet pussy. I gasped. He was a good, good size. He filled me up with his cock and he began to ride me, fuck me, fuck my brains out. I pushed back at him and wriggled and writhed and moaned and shook.

"Wrap those strong legs around me," he whispered in my ear before licking it. "Come on, wrap them around me."

I wrapped my legs around him and he went in

deeper. I gasped and he really began to fuck me. He overtook me. He took me over the edge and I began to come almost instantly. I squeezed my pussy around his cock and rode it until the orgasm stirred deep within me and then all I could do was hang on as it erupted inside my body, slowly at first and then with more force. He was coming and he was coming as hard as I was. The entire bed shook as we came and both of us grunted until it was all gone and there was nothing left to do but gasp for air.

After I stopped gasping, I realized what I'd just done. I turned to him and said, "I think you'd better go."

"Not just yet," he said and climbed back on top of me. "We've got more business to take care of."

I couldn't help but grin and wrap my arms around his neck and pull him in close to me. I muttered, "Well, if you insist."

"I insist."

I nodded. I might have insisted on it myself if he hadn't.

No pleasure without consequence.

As soon as Zack left, I was beside myself with anxiety and worry and pure and utter self loathe. I had just cheated. *Cheated.* I was a cheater! I was so bad. I was just like Tony! What I did was wrong. So wrong. I didn't know what to do. I paced the entire length of my house, smoked a half pack of cigarettes and cursed myself. Why had I done that? Why hadn't I sent him away? Why did I have to fall? Why had he been so chivalrous? Why did it feel so good?

Since I wasn't getting anywhere with myself, I called Tony.

"Hey, what's up?" he asked.

"Are you sitting down?"

"I am not sitting down," he said slowly. "What's wrong?"

"Tony," I said and took a deep breath. "I just cheated on Wes."

"I knew you would do it!" he exclaimed.

I was taken aback. I told him so.

"No," he said. "You're not getting off so easy, little lady. Admit it."

"Admit what?" I asked annoyed as hell at him.

"Admit what I was saying is true."

"And what was that?" I asked and tapped my foot.

"That people want to fuck around and it doesn't really have anything to do with loving the other person."

Fuck! He was right! Damn him!

"So, anyway," I said. "How's it going?"

"Not going to admit it, are you?"

"Listen, what I did was wrong, Tony. I know that and I just wanted to ask for you advice. Do you think I should—"

"No," he said, cutting me off. "Don't tell Wes."

I was aghast. "Why *not?*"

"Do you want trouble?"

"No," I said. I definitely did not want trouble. But I had started it so I would have to face some sort of consequence for it, right? No pleasure without consequence. Right. I hoped I was wrong.

"Katrina," he said as if he were humoring me. "I wasn't going to tell you when I had my affair. But then I started feeling guilty. So I told you and now I wished I hadn't."

"Fuck, Tony," I snapped. "This isn't about us."

"No, I don't suppose it is, but in retrospect, I wished I had just kept my mouth shut."

"Why?" I asked.

"Because I hurt you and I never wanted to do that."

"So why did you tell me?" I asked.

"Because I knew it would make me feel better," he said. "It was a selfish thing to do."

I was stumped.

"So," he said. "Just forget about it. Don't tell him. Move on with your life and pretend it never happened."

An image of Zack and me doing it doggie came to me. How in the hell was I supposed to I forget about *that?*

"Are you sure?" I asked. "Because I'm not so sure."

"I'm sure."

I left it at that. He was right. So, I kept it to myself. When Wes called later that evening, I told him about falling, but left out the part about Zack driving me home. I left out a lot of other things, too, but, hey, Tony told me it was the best way.

I was beginning to believe it, too.

"Do you need me to come over?" Wes asked, all concerned.

He was too good for me. I was such a louse! But it wasn't my fault. It was Zack's fault. No, it was all because of those damn dirty thirties. I just couldn't control myself anymore. Maybe I needed drugs.

"No," I heard myself saying. "That's okay. I just need to rest."

"Okay, sweetie," he said nicely. "Call me if you need anything."

"I will," I said and made sure to add, 'I love you."

I could tell he smiled. "I love you, too, baby."

Not an hour later, a big basket of flowers arrived from Wes. The card read: *Get well soon! You know how horny I am!*

I fell to the floor and wanted to kill myself. *Louse!*

Instead, I went to bed early and tried to ward off any sexual fantasies about Zack. Not an easy task considering he had fucked me two ways to Sunday. I tossed and turned and then couldn't stand it anymore and had to get out my vibrator and get happy before I could sleep.

I woke up several times during the night with a sense of dread coming over me. I tried to shake it off but couldn't. I knew I had just fucked up something so sweet and delicious with Wes. But I was human! That didn't make me a bad person!

Or did it...

I groaned and got up out of bed and started to get ready for the day. Wait a minute. I didn't have to get ready for the day. I'd called work and they told me to take as much time as I needed, that they'd reschedule all my appointments and to let them know if there was anything they could do.

Yeah, there was *something* they could do. They could give me my clean conscience back, that's what they could do. But they couldn't. I hated having a guilty conscience.

I went back to bed and hid under the blankets for a while. I tried to fall asleep but couldn't. I was such an early bird. Well, no sense lying there awake. I figured that I should at least brush my teeth. I did that and then started to walk into the kitchen for some orange juice when I heard a horn honk. I looked out the window and saw Zack pulling into my driveway in my little convertible. Oh. Shit. I had forgotten about my car! It had been at the gym since yesterday! I had also forgotten about him telling me he'd drive it home for me. I'd given him my keys without hesitation.

In less than two seconds, he was knocking on the door. I wasn't about to let him in. If I let him in, then…well, *that* would probably happen again. So, he was staying outside that damn door. And I was going to have him banned from the gym, too. He was way too much temptation for me.

I kept the door chained and opened it just enough to hold my hand out and said flatly, "Give me my keys."

"What's up with you?"

"You're not coming in here," I said calmly. "Now give me my keys."

"Why can't I come in?" he teased.

"Because you're a bad man," I said. "Now give me my fucking keys."

He chuckled and said, "What makes me a bad man?"

I groaned and said, "I think you know. Keys—give me my keys. Please."

He slipped them through the crack and said, "How are you feeling?"

"Why are you here?" I asked.

"I came to doctor you," he said and grinned. "And to bring you your car."

"Zack," I said. "I'm engaged."

"You don't have to be," he told me and slid his hand in and grabbed my arm. I shivered just from his touch, from that ultra light, but firm grip he had on me.

"Stop it," I said and wriggled away from him.

"Open the door."

"Zack, I can't see you."

He shrugged. He wasn't going anywhere. Not after that. Not after what we did yesterday. He wanted a repeat. So did I. But I couldn't. It wasn't allowed.

"Come on, baby," he whispered. "I just want to check your knee."

Well, in *that* case. I just stared at him. *No.*

"And I brought you a little something," he said and pulled a little gold box of chocolates out of his jacket. Oh, my God. He was too good. But so was Wes. Why couldn't I have both of them? One sent flowers, one chocolates. Together, they were more than perfect. I would never want for another thing in my life if I had both of them.

I stood my ground and told him, "You have to leave."

"Don't you want your chocolates?" he asked and shook the box.

I snatched the box out of his hand and said, "Thanks. Now leave."

"I will after you let me see your knee."

I was wavering. I really wouldn't mind him checking it out. It was swollen and blue today and it still hurt. I had to take care and not walk too fast or I might pop the kneecap right off. Didn't want that. He might be able to give me some pointers on how to keep the swelling down.

"Okay," I said and unchained the door. "But then you have to leave."

He came through, swept me up in his arms and carried me all the way to the bedroom. I screamed and yelled and fought him the whole way.

As he put me on the bed, he said, "Calm down. I have to have you lying down to check it."

I glared at him. "I don't like you man-handling me. And we're not playing doctor here!"

"I like to play doctor," he muttered and bent down to inspect my knee which was covered by my pajama bottoms and said, "Take off your PJ's."

"No way!" I snapped. "Now get out of here."

Of course, I was just acting angry. If he left, I would have chased after him. But I didn't want him to know I wanted it or anything. He'd have to work for it.

Thankfully, he ignored me, bent over me and in one swift motion, the bottoms were off and on the floor. And he was staring at my knee and at my black panties. He wriggled his eyebrows and said, "Oh, those are sexy."

God! That pissed me off. Like I had worn them for his benefit or something! Maybe I *had*, but still. I jumped up and began to beat my fists on his back. He allowed me for beat him for a moment and I could tell he was trying not to laugh. That pissed me off even more.

"Get out!" I yelled at him and tried to push him off the bed. "Now!"

"Keep that up and you'll have to be spanked."

He did not. *No.* He did not just say that to me! The bastard! I was about to hit him again but he caught my hand, flipped me over and I was suddenly aware that I was across his lap and he was spanking me! Like I was some little kid! Like I had done something bad!

Maybe he was my Karma.

I yelled, "Stop it, you pig!"

"How about a little spank?" he said. "Oh, she likes to be spanked."

Actually, it was kinda nice, I mean… No! I didn't like this. No one had ever done this to me and I hated that he was doing it now. The bastard! He was slapping my ass, spanking me. *Why was he doing this?*

I knew why.

"Zack!" I screamed. "Stop it!"

He gave me one last whack and said, "Did you like that?"

"You fucker!" I hissed. Actually, no I didn't like it. It stung like hell. But it felt kinda nice, too. I wouldn't let him know that. I rubbed my ass and groaned, "Why'd you do that? It hurt!"

He bent down and began to kiss and lick the places he slapped. Then he slapped it again. This time harder.

"Ow!" I said.

"Just wait."

"For what?" I asked. "For you to make me black and blue?"

"No, crybaby," he said. "Just wait."

I waited and he gave me another slap. This time, it felt…different. It felt…sexual. Something stirred within me. I felt it stir and then I felt myself, my pussy, grow warm, hot even.

"Feel it?" he whispered.

I nodded and he gave me another slap, this one got my juices flowing. I shuddered with passion.

"Oh, that little ass," he said and bent to kiss it. "It's so perfect. I love your ass."

"Zack—"

"Shh," he told me. "I'm talking."

I shut my mouth and waited.

"Your ass looks so damn good," he said and ran his hand over it. "I love your ass."

I lay there and tried to contain myself, tried to control myself. It took everything I had to not jump up, push him back on the bed and fuck his brains out. But I waited. There was something cool about to happen soon.

"I'm going to fuck your ass, baby," he said and grabbed it, squeezed it and then ran his hand between its cheeks. "I'm going to fuck it. Would you let me fuck your ass?"

He didn't even have to ask.

"Yeah, you'd like that, wouldn't you?" he whispered and pulled my shirt up and began to kiss my back. "What else would you like me to do?"

"Just what you're doing," I breathed.

"Oh, this?" he asked and began to play with my ass. "You like that? Are you a dirty girl? Tell me you're a dirty girl."

I couldn't believe I was saying the words as they came out of my mouth, "Yes, I'm a dirty girl."

"I thought you were," he said and slapped my ass, this time harder than before. He pushed me up on the bed and got between my legs and began to eat me, slurp at me, fuck me with his mouth and tongue. I laid there and shuddered, loving it all, loving the way he was doing it, loving that it was dirty and nasty and felt so good. I felt the first orgasm almost instantly and wailed a little. It felt so good I had to bite at my fist to keep from screaming.

Without a word, after I was finished, he positioned himself behind me, opened my legs and drove it in. He drove his hard cock right up in me as I lay there and panted and felt pain and passion and pure, unadulterated lust coming out of me. I felt it in my pussy and I felt it in my ass as he fucked me there. He grabbed the back of my head and pulled me to him so he could suck on my neck as he fucked me, as he fucked me in this dirty but ultimately satisfying way.

I moaned and found my hand between my legs, resting on my clit. I began to hump my hand. His hand went to my pussy and he fingered me there as I fingered myself as he fucked my ass. Then I felt it, this enormous orgasm. It began to tickle me, taunt me and it was coming at me from all over. My entire body, my entire being just felt it. Just felt alive and active, like every single cell in my body was being raised and told to tingle. I couldn't contain myself. I was lost then, lost inside that orgasm, so lost that it was controlling me, as I lost control. I began to howl like a wild animal and the sound ripped out of my throat and came out like a mad cry. And it was madness; it was so good it was almost dark and scary. And he began to cry out, too, but not in the same manner as me, but because he was about to come. No, he was coming as I was coming. We were both coming at the same time and each of use felt each other, each other's bodies and mind and souls and desires at that instant. And we fucked like that until neither of us could hold onto it anymore and we collapsed to the bed, with him lying on top of me.

"Damn," he said. "That was good."

I nodded but couldn't speak. I was at a loss for words. And I was still out of breath. We *had* to do *that* again.

"Yeah," I breathed and snuggled in the crook of his arms. "It was."

He sighed and said, "I think I love you."

I froze.

"I do," he said.

"That's a little…sudden," I stammered and sat up. "What the hell do you mean by that?!"

He sat up and said, "I don't know. It just came out."

I glared at him. "Don't fuck with me."

"I'm not fucking with you," he muttered. "It's like I thought it but I said it too. It was weird."

"Listen," I said. "This is about sex. And that's all it's about."

"I don't know," he said. "It's different."

"No, it's not different, Zack," I said and jumped off the bed. "Don't make it different. I already have one boyfriend!"

He swallowed hard. "So? What's so special about him?"

"He's my boyfriend!" I said. "He doesn't have to be special!"

"What?"

"I mean," I said and grabbed my cigarettes off the nightstand. "I don't have to explain why he's special."

He looked away and nodded. "So I can't be?"

"What?"

"Special to you," he said and turned back to me.

"I didn't say that."

"You didn't have to," he said and got out of bed.

"Zack, don't," I said and grabbed his hand.

He jerked it back and hissed, "Listen, I don't go around saying shit like that. It just popped out, okay? You don't have to spit on it."

"I wasn't spitting on it!"

"Yeah, you were!" he yelled and bent to grab his pants.

"Zack, please, just listen. I—"

"I don't want to listen," he said.

I threw my cigarettes down and went at him,

grabbing him by the waist and stopping him. He allowed me to hold him for a moment before he pushed me away and I fell on the bed.

"You bastard!" I yelled and before I knew what I was doing, I had jumped on him and was beating the shit out of his back. I don't know why he inspired this little rage in me but I hated the fact that he was bigger and stronger than I was and that meant he could throw me around like a sack of potatoes. But at the same time, I loved it. Maybe I wasn't trying to hurt him, maybe I was trying to get him to put me in my place. So he could fuck me again.

He spun me around, threw me on the bed and tried to hold me off him. But I wasn't having it. I slapped at him until he grabbed my arms, pinned them behind my back and got in my face.

He hissed, "If I want to love you, I will. You can't stop me."

"You better let me go, you bastard!" I hissed and felt spit fly out of my mouth and onto his face.

He jerked his head to the side, faced me again and pressed his lips against mine, pushing me back on the bed. I tried to scream and struggled against him but there wasn't much I could do. He was one strong son of a bitch. We fought all the way to the bed, all the way down and in one quick motion, he kissing me, pushing me down and I was responding, letting it take me over. And then nothing mattered. It didn't matter because we were soon fucking.

It was a slightly vicious fuck, slightly maddening because we bit at each other as we panted with lust and anger. He pounded against me so hard I gasped. I pushed back against him, and then sucked at his mouth until it opened and then I sucked at his tongue. He moaned and I opened my eyes. He was staring at me. I stared back and we began to fuck, slowly fuck, slowing down to feel it, really feel it. I squeezed my pussy and sucked his dick more deeply into me. He moaned and held still so I could ride it, ride his hard cock until I felt something stir, then erupt, then explode inside me. Intensely it exploded and I bit down on his shoulder and he cried out in pain, in pleasure and he rode me harder and rode me until he came and there was nothing left to do but ride it out and then hold each other as the feeling of euphoria slowly faded away.

I noticed we didn't move one single inch away from each other. We stayed like that for a very long time and we stayed like that because it felt right not to move away, not to experience the shame that comes with finding our clothes and covering our nakedness and our souls.

He said, "I love you."

I turned to stare at him and though I felt bad about saying it, it felt right to do it, so, I had no choice and I couldn't deny my feelings. I had to say it because I felt it. So, I said, "I love you, too."

He smiled. He smiled because he knew it already. I'd just confirmed.

Plaything.

I decided that Zack, because he was so rich, was just bored and I was his plaything for a while. I would happily remain his plaything until he got tired of me and moved on to another plaything. I liked being his plaything. And because I was his plaything, I didn't have to give up Wes.

I was getting so good at denial, I was starting to scare myself.

Zack came by in the mornings and then I saw Wes at night. Because I had already fucked like crazy and was still turned on by it, but the time dinner was over, I was jumping on Wes. My hormones were out of control. The more sex I had, the more I wanted. No. The more I *had* to have. All I could say was thank God for the pill.

I was such a bitch. Bitch, bitch, bitch.

But what could I do? I had two great men and just let me say, that was a damn good feeling. I was so happy I was listening to Barry White all the time. I'd crank up his greatest hits and just feel good about everything. About life and love and sex. I felt good about my body and about the blue sky and about the warm, desert wind. I felt good about helping my clients at the gym. I felt good about smiling all the time and about being so happy.

I was one lucky bitch and I knew it. So, I rode it out. I devoured life like a person should devour it. I loved my life, I loved everything about it and that's because I was sated. I was getting satisfaction on all levels. Both of my men gave me just enough space so I wasn't going crazy trying to schedule them into my daily routines. And both fit perfectly into my life. It wasn't like I was neglecting Wes for Zack. Zack in the mornings and Wes at night. Sometimes Wes would go away for business and Zack and I had an occasional night together. Sometimes Wes stayed over and Zack knew if his car was in the drive not to come in. Wes got more attention from me and because I felt awful for cheating on him, I didn't pick fights and I made sure to agree to go to his favorite restaurants and to wear his favorite dresses.

The guilt was bad. But it didn't stop me. I couldn't help myself. It just felt right to have an affair with Zack just like it felt right for me to be with Wes. Sure, it was downright deceitful and not a nice thing to do, but I couldn't stop it. I'd prepare a speech for Zack, outlining all the reasons why he had to get out of my life, then he'd show up with a box of chocolates and I'd be back to square one.

Then I began to rationalize it. Why not play it out and see what happened? What *could* happen? Wes could find out and break up with me. Then I'd have Zack. Zack could get bored and then I'd just have Wes. Deep down, I wanted both of them. Selfish, I know, but that's what I wanted. So, I kept it a secret and was very cautious on all levels. I didn't want to hurt Wes anymore than I wanted Zack to stop coming over. But in the meanwhile, I was so happy about it all, I was in a perpetual state of bliss. It was not a bad place to be.

Well, I knew what was eventually going to happen

and it happened before I was ready for it. But doesn't it always?

One night, I had Wes over for dinner and I noticed he was being really quiet. Like he was mad about something. Dumb me, I didn't think the obvious. Maybe it was because I hadn't seen Zack that morning and I had a lot of other things on my mind. Maybe it was because I was still thinking it was too soon for anything to come to a head. Maybe it was because I was such a dumbass.

"So how was work?" I asked and smiled at him.

"Okay."

"Do you like the chicken?" I asked. "I marinated it then I grilled it. Like in that recipe I told you about."

"It tastes fine."

"Oh," I said and sighed. "I'm thinking about getting my hair cut. What do you think?"

"Leave it alone."

He always said that. *Don't cut your hair. It looks good. Leave it alone.*

"So," I said. "Wanna go see a movie later on?"

"Doesn't matter to me," he said and sat up straighter in his chair. "We could ask your boyfriend to come with us, if you like."

I didn't immediately get what he was getting at. No, I was a dumbass and thought he was joking, so I joked back, "And maybe we could ask your girlfriend, too. Have a little group sex or something."

He glared at me for a few moments before he spat, "Sure, except *I* don't have a fucking girlfriend."

That's when I knew something was up.

"What's wrong with you?" I asked.

"Damn it, Katrina," he hissed. "Don't you fucking play games with me."

"*What?*" I asked, getting slightly irritated. "What are you talking about, Wes?"

"I saw you!" he yelled.

"Saw me what?!" I yelled back.

"You and your boyfriend, that tall motherfucker!"

Oh, no…nooooooOOOOO! I was shocked beyond belief. Who? What? When? Where? *WHY!?* Why, why, why, oh fucking why?! Oh, shit. Shitmotherfuckingshit! All good things must come to an end. And usually they come to a bad, bad end.

"What are you talking about?" I asked, trying to look innocent. I knew of course. I knew he knew. The big question was how long had he known? And what was he going to do about it?

"You and that…that…" he said and angrily threw his napkin down on the table. "You and that motherfucker kissing on your porch at six yesterday morning!"

Oh, shit. I had allowed Zack to stay over if he promised to leave early. He was going to be out of town for a week or so and I had made an exception. An exception that apparently wasn't the wisest choice to make. It was my undoing.

"What were you doing here at six in the morning?!" I yelled.

"I came by to give you back your Barry White CD," he hissed.

Damn Barry White! Barry White was my undoing!

81

"I was going to put it in your mailbox and not wake the princess from her fucking beauty sleep! I didn't know the princess was already awake!"

"Don't patronize me!" I yelled.

"I'll do what I damn well please," he hissed and got up from the table and began to pace, throwing his arms around like a madman. "And here I thought you were working all these extra hours! Here I thought you were tired and that's why you didn't want to stay over at my place as much. Here I was feeling sorry for you! But the real reason you're so tired is because you've got another boyfriend!"

I felt like one hundred percent grade-A shit. Nevertheless, I exclaimed, "I don't have another boyfriend! You're my boyfriend!"

"Oh, please," he scoffed. "I just can't believe you're such a slut!"

I stared at him. He was really beginning to piss me off. Here he was telling me I was a slut because I liked having sex! What did that make him?

"Wait a minute!" I yelled back. "Don't you dare call me that! Just because I'm a woman and I like sex doesn't mean you can classify me as street trash!"

"Well, that's what you're acting like!" he hissed.

Oh, God! That flew all over me! I wanted to scratch his eyes out! I wanted to do him some damage, some real damage. So what if I liked fucking? Big deal. Better than being a prude. Prudes were miserable and I should know. I had played that part well in my marriage. Wifey shouldn't like sex. Wifey is good, kind and pure. Wifey knows the way to a man's heart is through his stomach and doesn't have anything to do with his dick. All lies to make all wives miserable. To make all us women feel like shit for being sexual beings. All lies made up by men to make us stay in our place. Don't get any ideas about being what you want or acting out your sexual fantasies because it's all about the man. And I had bought into it. I had bought into it so much, it had destroyed my marriage. Tony wanted me to be more sexual, I just couldn't. I had society on my back forcing me to be good. *What will the neighbors think?* Wes didn't understand because he was a man and men were never made to feel bad over liking sex. Why did men want to make us feel bad over it? It's not like men could do it by themselves unless they jerked off and, really, what was the fun in that? Wasn't doing it with a woman much better? Sure, they could do it with each other but most of them didn't want that. They wanted a woman to do it with, not a man. I mean, sex is usually about a man *and* a woman. It takes two to tango.

"I just can't believe you," he said and shook his head. "I just can't."

I was so over this shit. How dare he talk to me like that? I had broken out of my shell and was just coming into my own sexually. And there he was telling me it wasn't okay. It wasn't okay for me to want more sex. All I could have was sex with him. Just sex with him. Then… Then I remembered our conversation just after we got engaged. He couldn't be faithful. He didn't want to lie to me, all that shit he fed me. Bastard! *He* couldn't be monogamous, but he sure as hell wanted *me* to be. Can you say hypocrite three times fast? Hypocrite,

hypocrite, hypocrite!

"Well," I said calmly. "It *was* your idea."

"What do *you* mean?"

"Oh, you don't remember telling me you couldn't be faithful? And that you were sorry and all that shit but—"

"I didn't mean—"

I finished for him, "For me to do it."

He glared at me. "No, I meant in the future when our obsession with one another wears off."

"No, you meant when your obsession with *me* wears off."

He glared at me but didn't respond.

"Isn't that right?" I hissed. "You knew one day you would want someone else to fuck and wouldn't want a nagging wife and—"

He held up his hand and said, "Katrina, I've heard enough."

"Well, I'm not finished, you hypocritical bastard!" I screamed and knew I should have never admitted it to him. I should have stonewalled him. Denied everything, told him he was hallucinating or that he had gotten the wrong house, the wrong girl and the wrong man. God, this was getting a little too complicated. Here he was pissed off as hell and *he* was the one who brought up having sex with other people. Of course, he never said anything about me doing it, had he? Oh, no, and why would he?

Of course, I had been the one to "talk" him out of it. Boy, what a stupid move on my part! I just didn't have any idea it could be as sweet as it was. But now I knew and I couldn't live without it. If that made me selfish, then that's what it made me. I wasn't going to start denying myself. I'd done that for years and for what? So I could be miserable? Fuck misery and fuck Wes if he didn't understand.

"It doesn't make it right," he said.

"It's not about right, Wes," I told him. "It's about you being a hypocrite."

"I am not a hypocrite!"

"From where I'm standing, it looks like you are."

His eyes shot bullets at me. I almost felt them. We stopped speaking. One of us would make a move. We were waiting the other out. One of us would have to make the decision to leave. That would be Wes. It was in his hands. One of us would try to make up. That would have to be me and I wasn't about to. Sure, it had been wrong, but it hadn't been *that* wrong.

"I've had enough," he hissed. "But I've got one more thing to do."

I watched as he stomped out of the dining room, heading to the bedroom. What was he going to do? Was he going to…? No. He wouldn't do that. He might!

I jumped up and raced after him. He already had my wedding dress out of the closet and was ripping it to shreds.

"What are you doing?" I wailed.

"What do you need with this?" he asked. "You bitch!"

"You motherfucker!" I screamed. "I paid for that!"

"I won't let you keep it so you can marry that asshole in it!" he roared. "I'd rather die!"

"That's mine!" I cried and grabbed what was left of it. I held it in my arms and began to sob. It was ruined, just like our relationship. I watched in horror as he stomped over to me, grabbed my hand and yanked my engagement ring off my finger. He took it, threw it to the floor and smashed it to bits.

It was really over. Nothing I could do about it now. How did things get so complicated? Why does sex complicate everything? Why does it make everything bad and ugly? It shouldn't. It should be revered. It was the one thing in this world that made a person really and truly happy. And everyone shit on it. Everyone was so scared of it, of its power. And it had power over all of us and there wasn't a damn thing we could do about it but sit back and watch it tear our lives apart.

"Now how does that feel?" he asked.

I just stared at up at him with tears running down my face. "You're mean."

He got down in my face and hissed, "Yeah, now you know how I feel. Now you know how bad it hurt when you broke my heart."

"Wes—"

"Don't talk to me," he said and headed out of the bedroom. "Ever again."

And with that he left. And I with that, my heart felt dead. I didn't know how I was ever going to recover.

Nothing to do but sit back and cry. And I cried for two days. Not just over Wes and our failed relationship, but because of what broke us up. I didn't hate him. Even though could have, really easily. My feelings could have turned black. But I didn't want to ruin what we had by coloring it with hate. He didn't single-handedly ruin it and neither did I. It just got complicated. Forced to look at what we were really all about, neither of us could handle it. The world was bigger than we were and once we stepped outside of our world, it came crashing down on us.

What if the shoe had been on the other foot? What if he had been the one to cheat? I knew I would have taken it badly. I would have cried and broken up with him, the same way that Tony and I had broken up. But then, I knew I would have moved on from it. *If* I felt like I felt now. If I knew what I knew now. Sex isn't bad. Having sex and loving other people isn't bad. What's bad is confronting that feeling of knowing you are not the only person in the world who can give another person all his good feelings. Knowing others can do it too is like a shot to the heart. That's where all the trouble comes in. That's where it all starts. We're so afraid of losing ourselves to someone else that when we do, we become frightened that they will take that love away. And the thought of having them lose themselves to someone besides us is terrifying. It makes us bitter and hateful. We gave it all to them and then they gave it to someone else.

But the thing was, I didn't take any love away from Wes to give to Zack. I loved both of them. I never knew I could love like that. There was so much love in me. I sometimes felt like I could burst from it.

On the third night after Wes left, he banged on the door. I almost didn't let him in. I almost pretended not to be home. But I knew we'd have to confront each other at least one more time. There was no way around it. So I let him in.

He didn't speak for a very long time and neither did I. We just sat on opposite ends of the couch and stared at the TV, which was turned off.

"I don't know what to say to you," I said finally.

He nodded but didn't reply.

"But I am sorry I hurt you," I said and stared at him. "I never wanted to hurt you."

"Didn't you think I'd find out?" he muttered.

"Yeah," I said. "But I tried not to worry about it."

"What do you mean?"

"I mean," I said and swallowed hard. "I just wanted to live and whatever happened would happen without me forcing the issue."

"Is that right?" he asked, starting to get angry. "I just can't believe you."

"Believe me?"

He turned to face me. "I can't believe what a little slut you are."

This time, I succumbed to the anger. I couldn't stop myself. I was at him and on him and I had slapped him before I even knew what I was doing.

"You bastard!" I yelled and slapped him again. "How dare you?!"

He grabbed my hand and pulled me to him. "That's what you are, isn't it?"

"Yes," I hissed. "And fuck you!"

"Fuck me?" he snarled. "No, fuck you."

"Get out of here!" I screamed. "Now! We're over! Done! Through!"

"Why did you do it?"

"I'm human," I said. "I can't be loyal to just one man. I thought we discussed this already!"

"No, you didn't want to do that, as I remember," he said. "I changed for you and for what? So you could fuck around on me?"

"I'm sorry you feel that way," I said calmly. "Now get the fuck out of here."

"Is he coming over?"

"He has a name and it's Zack," I said. "And, though it's none of your damn business, he isn't coming over. He's out of town."

"So that's why you're alone."

"No," I said. "I'm alone because I choose to be alone tonight. Remember, I'm a little slut and I could go down to the bar and bring any old thing home if I wanted to."

"Yeah," he said, nodding. "That's true."

"Don't egg me on, motherfucker," I hissed, shaking with fury.

"Why not?" he asked. "You said it yourself, a little slut like you can go out and get fucked whenever you like."

"You're damn right I can," I said and suddenly felt myself lunge for him. He had me so pissed off I didn't even realize I was beating at his chest with my fists until he had me turned me around and pushed me up against the wall, my back to him. I couldn't believe he did that. I couldn't believe I was in that position. I was, all of a sudden, helpless.

"Wes, stop!" I yelled.

"No," he said calmly and his hand came around to unzip my jeans.

"Stop!" I yelled and pushed away from him and ran into the bedroom. He ran after me. I got to the bed and stopped, staring at him, feeling somewhat scared. What was he going to do? I could understand why he was so upset, to a certain degree, but this anger of his was something new. I'd never seen it before. And I didn't much like it.

"Isn't this what you want?" he asked and grabbed me and threw me to the bed.

"Wes!" I yelled and tried to crawl away from him. "Stop it!"

He flipped me over and climbed on top and the next thing I knew he was kissing me, kissing me viciously and dangerous and like he didn't care if I was enjoying it or not. But then I found myself responding to that hateful kiss but before I could moan and enjoy it, he flipped me over, pushed my hips up off the bed until I was on all fours and tore the clothes from my body. And then he fucked me. He fucked me hard, again like he didn't care if I was getting anything out of it but then at the same time he knew I was and I was because he was filling me up with his hard cock and just from that I was coming and he was coming and as he came, he pulled out and sprayed his hot and sticky cum all over my back. I shuddered as it hit me and felt myself returning from orgasm land. It was a good fuck, maybe too good. It was one of those fucks that sent a person over the edge and the edge is sometimes a scary place to be.

I fell to the bed exhausted. He fell down beside me and we stared at each other for a long moment, not speaking, not thinking, just staring and feeling what we really felt for one another, love. No matter what I did or what he said, we couldn't change our feelings.

"Do you love him?" he asked quietly.

"I don't know," I said. "But I do know I love you."

"Is he a fling?"

I thought about that. Was Zack a fling? I didn't know. I knew if he stopped seeing me tomorrow, I would be hurt. I would be okay with it, but it would hurt like hell. I had tried to guard my feelings for him and not feel any love but when you share what we'd shared—all that good, intense hot sex—it was hard not to love the person who was giving it to you. It just happened like that.

"I don't know, baby," I said and ran my finger down the bridge of his nose. "I don't want to lie to you."

He stared at me sadly.

"I mean," I said. "I like you both. I mean...I'm in love with you but with Zack, I really like him, too. I never thought I could feel like this about two men at the same time."

"But you do love me, right?"

"I do," I said and smiled at him. "I really, really do."

He nodded. "I'm sorry I was such an asshole."

"I accept your apology."

"No, I mean it," he said. "I hate that I hurt you."

"It's okay."

He shook his head and looked like he was on the verge of tears. He grabbed me and pulled me to him, kissing my cheek as he said, "I wouldn't hurt you for the world. I was just so jealous I couldn't see straight. I didn't even know I had it in me to be like that."

He was making me so sad. I felt tears stream down my cheeks. We were healing then, after we had hurt each other. It was a good feeling to heal together like that. It brought us closer to admit to each other the things we had admitted.

"Don't cry," he said and wiped my face with his thumb. "I can't stand to see you hurting like this."

"I'm not hurting so bad," I said. "I'm just feeling an enormous amount of love for you right now."

He seemed almost shocked. As if he didn't think I could ever love him after what he'd done. "Really? You feel love?"

I nodded. "I feel love. Lots of it."

He smiled, but then it disappeared as quickly as it came. "I am just so sorry."

I held his face with my hand and forced him to look into my eyes. "It's okay. It's understandable. I forgive you."

He nodded but shrugged. "I don't know what came over me. You know I would never hurt you, right?"

"I know."

He began to kiss me, kiss the tears off my face, kiss me everywhere, from my forehead to my breasts, to my legs. Soft kisses that made me tingle and want more.

He murmured something. I opened my eyes and stared down at him, kissing my feet. I said, "What?"

"What did it feel like?" he asked and stared back at me.

"What do you mean?"

He crawled up my body until we were nose to nose. "What did it feel like with him?"

Was he serious? Did he really want to know? What could I tell him? And if I told him, would he get upset again?

"It was okay," I lied, thinking that was the best route to go and smiled at him. "Not like what we do."

"Like we do?"

"Yeah," I said and wrapped my arms around his neck. "When we have sex, it's like we have a strong connection. A soul connection, like a soul fuck."

He stared at me and said, "I know what you mean. But I want to know what you felt when you fucked him."

"Just lust."

"If it was just lust," he said. "You wouldn't have let him spend the night."

That was true. But I didn't want to hurt him anymore. I wanted this to be over so we could resume our lives and get onto the living.

"You can tell me," he said and began to kiss me again. "You can tell me and I won't get mad."

His touches were becoming more concentrated and I felt them, I felt them teasing me, preparing me for the orgasm that lay ahead. I felt him bringing me under his control, like he always did whenever we were alone like this. And, as he did this, I began to feel freer and I began to tell him.

"It was hot," I muttered and felt embarrassed.

"Where did you do it?"

"On the bed."

"On this bed?" he asked and stared at it, then back at me.

I bit my bottom lip and nodded. "Yeah, here and once in the kitchen."

"On the table?" he asked and his hand went between my legs.

"No," I said. "On the floor."

"What did he do to you?" he asked and began to play with me, with my pussy which was so wet it was dripping.

"He gave me…" I stopped.

"What?"

"He kissed me down there."

"Like this?" he asked and pushed my legs open wider and gave my pussy one good long stroke with his tongue.

I shivered and muttered, "Yeah."

"Or did he do this?" he asked and pressed his mouth against it and his tongue came out and gave it another lick.

"Yeah, like that," I moaned and began to feel the orgasm.

"Or did he do this?" he said and pulled away from me and flipped me over. He grabbed my ass and raised it in the air and then pushed his cock inside me. It felt so good, I gasped.

"Yeah, like that," I moaned.

He gave a hard thrust and grabbed my head and pulled it to him. "Did he fuck you like this?"

"Yeah," I moaned. "He did."

He gave another thrust that sent me over the edge. I was *this* close to coming. I was so wound up I could have jumped off the bed and humped the leg of a chair. But I wasn't going anywhere. I didn't have to. He was going to give it to me.

"You like that, don't you?" he asked and began to ride me.

I held onto the bedpost and moaned, "Yeah, I do."

"Yeah, you like it," he said and didn't stop. "Tell me you like it."

"I like it," I moaned.

"How much?"

"A lot!" I gasped and began to come. I couldn't do anything then but hang on for the ride, hold onto him as we both began to come and we were coming hard. It was the most intense sex we'd ever had. So intense I was screaming with ecstasy and with pain. It hurt to fuck like that. But it was a good hurt.

One the orgasm began to trickle away, we fell to the bed and he grabbed me and pulled me into his arms. He began to kiss me and I lay there and kissed back. He stopped suddenly and eyed me.

"Are you still going to see him?" he asked.

"No," I said.

"Why?"

"Because I don't want to lose us."

He sighed. "You can still see him."

"Wes—"

"No, I mean it. You can still see him."

"But I don't want to," I lied. "I don't want to see him."

"You don't?"

I shook my head. "No, it hurts you too much."

"I'll get through it," he said. "And something like sex shouldn't break us up."

"But—"

"But if you're going to do this," he said, cutting me off again. "I want something."

"What?"

"I want to watch."

"What!" I screeched.

"You have to let me watch," he said.

My mouth fell open. "Are you kidding me?"

"No," he said and straddled me, squeezing my body between his legs. "I want to see what he does to you."

I couldn't believe what I was hearing.

"But more importantly," he said. "I want to see you. I want to see your face when you're getting fucked."

I was dumbfounded.

"Don't tell him I'm going to do it," he said. "I don't want him to know I'm here."

"I don't know if I can do that," I said and shook my head.

"You can," he said. "You can do anything you damn well please. A guy like me can't stop you."

"What does that mean?"

"It means," he said and kissed my nipple. "I want you to be who you are. I want you to be free. And once you're free, I can be free and we can be happier than we ever imagined."

"So this is about you, too?"

"It's about us," he said. "Me and you doing what we want to do and what I want right now is to see you get fucked."

I was stumped.

Comedy of errors.

Even as I was setting the "date" up with Zack, I couldn't believe I was doing it. I felt devious and weird. I don't know why I even agreed but I had, so I had to go through with it.

"Just relax," Wes said. "Don't even think about me being there. Okay?"

Now that was going to be hard. How could I *not* think about him being there? He was going to be in the closet like some damn peeping Tom for God's sake!

"This is how it will work," he said. "Invite him over here, bring him into the bedroom and do your thing. I'll watch from the closet and when you're done, make him leave."

He didn't know but when Zack came over, his visits weren't that short. We didn't do quickies.

"I don't know, Wes," I said. "This is just a little too weird for me."

"How is it weird?"

"Well, you're going to be in the closet like some pervert watching us and it's going to make me uncomfortable as hell."

"You don't understand," he said.

"Maybe I could just set up a video camera."

He seemed to like that idea, but then he shook his head. "No, I want to see the real thing."

"Why don't you just go to a sex club or something?"

"Because I want to see *you*, not some damn bimbo who's pretending she's getting off. I want to see you doing it."

"Me doing what exactly?"

"Damn it," he said, exasperated. "You getting off with another guy. I want to see what you look like while you're doing it. It's not about the act itself, it's about you."

Oh.

"It's like… Almost like you're my very own…"

"What?"

"Porno actress."

Really? Wow. I liked that idea but this was just mind boggling. I couldn't get around the fact that he wanted to see me like that. Especially after he had freaked out on me like he had. I didn't want another freak out.

"You can't freak out," I said. "If you see it and it pisses you off, you have to stay in that damn closet."

"I know," he said. "This is just as much for me as it is for you."

"Ya think?" I asked sarcastically and rolled my eyes.

"I have to get over this jealousy and I want you to

help me," he said and put his arms around my waist.

"This is just so weird," I said and shook my head at him.

"It feels weird now, but once you do it, it won't."

"How would you know?"

"I just do," he said.

What did that mean? Maybe he thought if I went through it, then it wouldn't be a big deal once it was over. I didn't know what the hell he meant. All I knew was that this was going to turn out bad. I felt it in my gut. How could it have turned out otherwise?

"Okay," I muttered and left it at that. I was still feeling guilty for fucking Zack in the first place and I guess I thought if I did what Wes wanted me to, then I could make it up to him. But this felt a little extreme.

I didn't even know why Wes wanted this. It was out of the blue. At first, he was livid with jealousy and now he was curious. I couldn't get my head around it but then decided he wanted to see it so he could cut me loose. Seeing me fuck some other guy would make him fall out of love with me. It would be easier that way.

I hated it. I hated the thought of it and I almost hated Wes for putting me in this position. Even if I'd brought it on myself.

I almost considered telling Zack about it, just so he'd know, but, sensing my doubt, Wes said, "And don't tell him anything abut it. He might not be able to get it up if you do."

"What are you? A sex expert or something?"

"I've read a few books," he said.

Whatever. I guess I should have a read a few books

myself. I just hoped it turned out alright. I didn't want Zack to feel like he was on display or something and I hoped he would never know what I had set up.

The big day finally arrived. Zack came over to my house right at noon, like he always did on Wednesdays. Wes had taken the day off for this special occasion. I was almost mad at him over all this. It was getting too complicated and like I said, it was just a little too weird for me. What if this happened and what if that happened? It was truly going to end up being a comedy of errors. I could almost hear the canned laughter as I imagined Zack and Wes confronting each other. "No, I'm her boyfriend," they'd both say right before I came in and got caught in the middle. *Argh!*

But I had agreed and I couldn't back out. I might as well do it and let the chips fall where they may. I just hoped they didn't fall on me. I could see how this might work out badly. I could see Wes storming out of the closet and taking Zack by surprise. I just see them beating the shit out of each other. They were both large men, both over six foot and both muscular as hell. That thought brought some sexy imagines to my head. Divine. They were both so damn divine. If I could just have both of them…

What? What was that? No. I never wanted one of those. I never even considered having a threesome. But now I was considering it and it sounded almost like a good idea. No, I wasn't. I wasn't *that* into sex. No, not me. I mean, who would want that? I stopped myself but the fantasy of both of them giving it to me came hard and I almost fell over with lust. I saw both of them pawing at me, grabbing at my body, kissing me, fucking me.

I wanted it. I was that into sex.

I shook myself. No. That would never happen. Things like that only happened in porno movies. And this wasn't a porno movie. This was my life. And after this was all said and done, I had a distinct feeling it was going to suck bad.

Zack came over promptly at noon. He came with another box of chocolates which he knew I couldn't eat. I mean, I was a personal trainer and if I got fat, I would lose my job. I appreciated the thought even though I'd have to throw them in the garbage. Just where our relationship/fling was going to go after today.

I mean, this couldn't work out right. It just couldn't. It had disaster written all over it. Any fool could see it from a mile away. *Danger, danger, leave premises immediately! Odd sexual behavior going on!*

Zack kissed my cheek and said, "You look absolutely beautiful today."

I blushed. It embarrassed me whenever I got compliments like that. Thanks. You don't look so bad yourself.

"Thanks," I said and let him into the house. "How are you today?"

He grabbed me, pulled me into his arms and said, "I'm horny, baby."

I laughed nervously and said, "Well, you came to the right place."

"I always do and I come the right way," he said and laughed at his dumb joke. I didn't laugh. Usually his dumb jokes cracked me up mainly because he was the one telling them. He got a slightly wicked twinkle in his eyes whenever he told one and then would wait in anticipation to see if I would laugh. I never laughed at the joke, but I laughed because he wanted me to laugh. He cracked me up, not the jokes. But today, I couldn't have laughed if my life depended on it.

"Oh," I said.

He smiled and bent to kiss me. I couldn't relax at first but then I did and started to get into it. I responded and tried to steer him over to the couch.

"No," he whispered. "Let's go into the bedroom."

Oh, boy. Here it was. Step to it.

"Okay," I said a little high-pitched. I cleared my throat and said, "Okay. Let's go."

He grabbed my hand and led me into the bedroom, pushed me back on the bed and began to kiss me through my clothes. I lay there stiffly, staring at the closet door, which Wes was peeking out of. I just felt weird, odd. I couldn't relax.

"What's wrong?" he asked and stared into my eyes. "Did I do something wrong?"

"No."

"Then what is it?"

"Nothing," I muttered and stared at the wall.

He kissed my cheek and said, "Come on, tell me."

I stared at him and felt like crying. This was so

overwhelming for me. I couldn't get past it to enjoy myself. Wes was the one with the weird problem, not me. It wasn't my fault I couldn't relax and enjoy what Zack wanted to give me. And he wanted to give it to me so badly. I just couldn't allow myself to take it. That was being too selfish and maybe a little weird.

"Come on, baby," he said. "Tell me what's wrong."

"I'm just stressed out," I said.

"Poor baby," he muttered. "We don't have to do anything. We can just lay here and hold each other."

"No!" I said a little too shrilly, then calmed down. "No, I mean, we can do stuff."

"Are you sure?" he asked. "I just want to make sure you're in the mood is all."

"I'm sure," I said and smiled weakly. "Come on."

I rose up off the bed and pressed my lips against his, but I didn't feel the initial little shock of excitement, of pleasure, I normally did. He didn't seem to notice and began to kiss me.

I responded at first but I kept thinking about Wes staring at us and I couldn't get into it. I was so nervous that nothing felt good, nothing felt *right*. But what if... What if I told him that Wes was in there? What if I made Wes come out and confess that we'd set this up? It couldn't be any worse than this feeling of loathing I had. And I had it. I felt like I was deceiving Zack and I didn't like that feeling at fucking all.

I took a chance. "Hold on."

"What?" he asked and his eyes narrowed at me.

"Just sit tight," I said and went to the closet and opened the door all the way. "Come out, Wes."

No answer. This really was threatening to become a comedy of errors.

"Come on, Wes," I said and looked in the closet. He wasn't there! Where was he? I looked around the room, and then focused on the bathroom door. He was in the bathroom.

"What are you doing?" Zack asked suspiciously.

I stared at him and thought about laughing it off. But then what? I had to tell him. I hated to lie, to be devious. It just wasn't in my nature.

"What kind of game is this?" he asked and came over to me.

"It's not a game," I said. "I—"

He cut me off by kissing me and then he took me over, took control of me. The next thing I knew, he had my skirt hiked over my hips and was going down on me. I couldn't stop myself from enjoying that. I draped my leg over his shoulder and got into it, got into the cool but sweet sensations his tongue and mouth and salvia were giving me.

I glanced over at the bathroom. No movement. Maybe Wes had left. Maybe he had crawled out the window. I didn't know but I did know I was about to have a little orgasm. It came at me and devoured me, then went away as quickly as it came. I shuddered and Zack pushed me up against the wall and I helped him unzip his pants and put his cock inside me. He fucked me standing up, up against the wall and before I knew what was happening, I was coming again. I was so caught up in the moment and the idea of someone watching—of Wes watching—was actually beginning to turn me on. I could just feel his eyes on me, devouring me the way that Zack was devouring me then, with his lips and hands and dick. I stared towards the bathroom and suddenly wanted him in there, watching me get off.

"Ahh," Zack moaned and came inside me. He gave a few more thrusts before kissing me. "That was so good, baby."

"I know," I said and kissed him back.

"Give me a minute and we'll do it again."

I stared at him and nodded, then looked over his shoulder and gasped. Wes was standing there behind us, staring at us, staring at us still joined together. And we stared at each other and both of us felt something shift in our relationship, in our hearts and in our souls. It was acceptance of me being sexual, of me being a woman and him being a man. Acceptance of both of us for what we were. This was why he wanted it, to show me how it could be, how good it could be. I was so overcome with emotion, I almost started crying.

"What is it?" Zack asked and looked over his shoulder. He saw Wes and his mouth dropped open, then he stared back at me. "What the hell is going on here?"

Before I could answer, Wes was at Zack and I just knew he was going to start a fight. But he didn't. He grabbed him by the shoulder and literally pulled him off me and then he was on me, kissing me, devouring me. I responded before I could help myself. Maybe it was because that lust I felt, that lust which surged though my body. I wanted to share that lust. I moaned and ate at his mouth as he ate at mine, then he was eating at my breasts. Then he was fucking me just like Zack had done a minute or so earlier. I don't know what Zack did, or what he was thinking. I was just overcome by Wes and couldn't think of anything besides his fucking me and me fucking back and my next orgasm which was right there in front of me, dangling closely, letting me know I could reach for it at any time. I grabbed it and came, just like *that*. All the lust I had ever felt seemed to seep inside of me at that moment I came and I have never felt such liberation as I did then.

Wes came with a grunt and a groan and then he pulled my head back and thrust his tongue in my mouth, kissing me hard. I kissed back and moaned as the orgasm finally left me, leaving its mark all over my body, which was red and ready for another round.

Zack was staring at us. I kissed Wes and stared back. I wanted him too, I wanted him again. Right now. Something inside me had been awakened and I was ready for it to take me to the next level.

Zack shook his head and started out of the room.

"Don't go," I said. "I can explain."

"You don't have to," he muttered.

I moved away from Wes and ran after him, grabbed his hand and said, "Listen to me. I don't know what to say, but—"

"You don't have to say anything. I understand."

"You do?"

"Yeah," he said and glanced at Wes. "He gets off watching you fuck other guys. I was one of the other

106

guys."

"No!" I exclaimed. "It's not like that."

"Looks like that to me."

I turned to Wes for help. "Tell him Wes."

"It's true," Wes said and cleared his throat. "This was the first time."

Zack stared at him like he didn't believe him.

"Really," I said. "He saw us together one day and he got really pissed off but then he wanted to... And I'm sorry if you don't like it or whatever, but..." I stopped. I really didn't know what to say.

"But," Zack said. "I thought you and I had something special."

"We do," I said. "We can."

"But you're with him," he said and jerked his head over to Wes. "And that means you can't ever be with me."

"That's not true," I said.

"Listen," Wes said. "It was just a once in a lifetime thing. It's over now. I apologize if it made you uncomfortable."

"Made me uncomfortable?" Zack said and pointed at himself. "Yeah, you could say that!"

"Zack, it's not like that," I said and held his arm tighter. "Just—"

"Leave me alone," he said and shoved me away from him, shoved me so hard, I fell to the floor and felt like a fool.

Then my worse fear came true. Wes was on Zack in a second and they were fighting, kicking, punching the shit out of each other.

"Stop it!" I screamed and tried to tear them apart. "Stop it now!"

But they weren't stopping. They were going to beat the life out of one another. I sat there and watched numbly and wondered what I could do. Wes was now punching Zack in the face. After he got a couple of punches in, Zack grabbed his arm and gave him a good one back. I was almost in awe of this fight. It was the best I'd ever seen. And, I hate to admit it, but it turned me on beyond belief. These two strong men fighting over me. Oh, God. Those muscles. I couldn't watch for long or there would be nothing left of either one of them, so I did what I had to do.

I threw my head back and screamed at the top of my lungs. Screamed until I was hoarse and screamed until they stopped fighting and just stared at me. When I finally stopped, I couldn't speak my throat was so dry.

Zack got up and fetched me a glass of water and Wes rubbed my back.

"Are you okay?" he asked with concern.

I shook my head and grabbed the water out of Zack's hand and downed it.

"Are you going to be alright?" Zack asked.

I held one finger up and he clamped his mouth shut. When I got my voice back I said, "You two have really got a lot of nerve."

They just stared at me.

"You're fighting over me like I'm a piece of meat," I hissed though I was far from being pissed off. I was too turned on to be pissed off. I couldn't let them know that, though.

They dropped their heads.

"I mean, come on," I said and pulled my skirt down. "Where do you get off?!"

Wes started to say something but I held my hand up and he shut his mouth.

"Uh uh," I snapped and resumed pacing. "I agreed to do this, Zack, because Wes was so overcome with jealousy that he couldn't see straight. Sorry, but that's why. No, we've never done this before and if you think we're a bunch of perverts, then fine. I don't give a shit."

He nodded and glanced at Wes, then down at the floor.

I turned to Wes. "And I agreed to do this for you. *You!* And you repay me by beating the shit out of him? Who do you think you are?"

He shrugged and looked ashamed. Good enough for him.

"I am not going to put up with this shit," I said. "We're here now and whatever that means, then that's what it means. Sorry, life works like this sometimes. You do crazy things and sometimes they work out and sometimes they backfire."

They nodded simultaneously.

"Now I'm going to take a shower," I said and turned on my heel. "If you like, we can talk some more when I'm done."

As soon as the warm water hit me, I began to calm down. And I began to think about them, both of them giving it to me. The idea was divine and sexy. It was a little too much and in a matter of minutes, I had convinced myself if I could get them both to fuck me at the same time, then all of this could be over. I could also give this whole threesome thing a try and see what all the fuss was about.

I got out of the shower and wrapped a towel around my body then went back into the bedroom. Wes was sitting on the bed and Zack was in a chair. They weren't talking or looking at each other. I could feel the tension. I was determined to change it and make it all better, for all three of us.

"Now," I said and clapped my hands together. "We can do one or two things. We can leave this room and forget it ever happened. Or we can move on and do it the right way."

"What?" Wes asked.

"If we're going to do this, we're going to do it the right way," I said. "And that means, both of you are going to fuck me at the same time."

They weren't the least bit shocked. Well, they were a little but I could tell the idea was just as intriguing to them as it was to me. I took the towel off and stood before them naked and as their eyes drank me in, I felt a surge of sexual power wash all over me and give me the courage to do this. I felt like such a woman then, naked but in control. I had what they both wanted. And that made me want this.

I went over to the bed and lay down. "Wes, come over here."

He came over and sat down beside me.

"Come on, Zack," I said and watched him walk over and sit on my opposite side. "Now sit back and relax and let's see how this goes."

"Katrina," Wes said. "Are you sure you want to do this?"

"Yeah, I am," I said. "And I want to see if you two can do it as well. You think you got the balls?"

They glanced sideways at each other and nodded.

To be honest, I didn't know if I could go through with it. I could tell that our first ménage a trois was going to be nerve wracking. I was apprehensive because I'd never done anything like that and I was more than sure they hadn't either. What if I pissed one of them off? What if I upset one of them by doing something the other had never seen before? If I kissed Zack first would that make Wes jealous?

I tried not to think about it and just did what felt right.

I offered Wes my mouth and Zack my pussy. Both seemed pleased with my decision and responded accordingly. I took Zack's hand and pushed between it my legs and then I pressed my lips against Wes's. His mouth opened and as our tongues touched, a deep moan came out of my lips. I was so turned on. I felt Zack's hand between my legs, touching me and exploring my pussy, fingering me. He got between my legs and pulled them open and he dove in, beginning to lick and suck and kiss at me.

Wes moved back and I unzipped his pants, grabbed his cock and began to suck at it as Zack sucked at me. I loved having it in my mouth as I was being eaten. The two sensations were thrilling. I tasted Wes's precum and I could feel myself about to orgasm.

I stared down at Zack and said, "Put it in me."

He nodded and pulled it out and pushed his hard cock inside me, filling me up and as he concentrated on fucking me, I concentrated on Wes whose head was thrown back with a look of ecstasy on his face. I smiled because then I had both of them in my control, both of them by the balls. Both of them inside of me in different but similar ways.

Zack's fucking became more concentrated and I began to focus on Wes more. I could tell if I gave a little more effort to Zack I would have come really quickly. But I wanted this to last. Both of their hands were on me. Zack had his face buried in my neck and he was kissing it and sucking on it. Wes was squeezing my breast with his hand and all the sensations mingled in the exact right way and it was overpowering. Before I could stop myself, I was coming and so was Wes. His hot cum just shot into my mouth just and I sucked him dry as I came, slurped it up and wanted more.

Zack came just then and grunted as he filled my pussy up with himself, with his hot cum. I loved that feeling. I loved the dirtiness of all of this. Of getting off because you were horny and doing it because it felt good to do it. We were doing it for the pleasure of doing it. And it was a pleasure to do it.

When it was over, we fell away from each other. I noticed they didn't really look at each other. Not that much. But I couldn't take my eyes off them. Damn, they were so hot.

Wes got up and lit me a cigarette. As I smoked it, I inhaled with satisfaction and wondered when we could do it again. I was so lost in my thoughts that I didn't hear something Zack just said.

"What'd you say?" I asked.

Zack said, "We should do this again.

Wes agreed by nodding. "I mean, if you want to, Katrina."

I grinned and couldn't believe my luck. Did I want to? Were they crazy? Of course I wanted to and I wanted to as soon as I finished my cigarette.

So we did.

Double the pleasure.

So it began. So it was. About once a week, we'd meet up and have a three-way. It was so damn good. I never thought anything like it was possible. But it was. And it was happening to me.

"I have an idea," I said and smiled at Wes and Zack. "Wanna hear it?"

They nodded.

I pulled the scarf from behind me and held it up with one finger. "How about it?"

Wes got my meaning and took the scarf. He and I had done this sort of thing before. Once he even tied me to the bed. So, with a smile, he wrapped it around my head, thusly covering my eyes.

Oh, *y-e-sssss!*

He pushed me back on the bed and I felt Zack lay down next to me. And then I had four hands all over my body, giving me tasty sensation after tasty sensation until I couldn't take it anymore. I moaned and felt one of their mouths on my wet pussy. I moved a little and decided it was Wes down there. Each of them had a distinct technique.

Hands all over me. Hands in my hair, tracing lines across my face, across my belly, across my breasts. Hands teasing me, bringing me intense pleasure.

One of them turned me over and my ass was in the air and I knew, just knew what they were going to do. They were going to give me double the pleasure. They were going to double penetrate me. We had never talked about it and we pretended not to think about it. I had always wondered *when* they would do it. I had never wondered *if.*

To be honest, I didn't know if I could take it. But I didn't have much choice. I wouldn't know which orifice either of them would take, but I had a feeling Wes would take my pussy and Zack would take the other less charted area. He and I had done that only once but I knew we'd do it again. Today seemed to be the day.

Wes fucked me for a long minute which made my juices flow even more and then I felt the Zack's dick. It was slowly easing into me. It took its time, took time to take care, to make sure it wasn't a sudden entry, a sudden jerk which might bring me pain. No, it wanted to make sure it was *all good.*

And it was. It was all good. Zack's hard cock was almost all the way in and combined with Wes's hard cock and the intensity of the moment, I could barely do anything but pant. It was all this feeling, all this feeling combined with just a touch of pain, which soon eased into euphoria as I realized I was going beyond the limits. I was doing something purely for the pleasure of doing it and it was such a deep, intense pleasure, I didn't know why I hadn't tried it before.

They began to fuck me then, both of them, at the same time. I had both of them in me simultaneously, together, and that thought of having both of them turned me on beyond belief. Fucking me like the woman I was; fucking me like the men they were. The strong men who wanted nothing but to bring me pure satisfaction, pure delight. They liked doing that to me; they liked fucking me like I was a piece of meat. I liked being a piece of meat. It added to the dirtiness and made me feel more human, more vulnerable, more susceptible to pleasure.

I don't know how long it went on, the fucking, all I know was that I couldn't get enough. It was the most intense sexual experience I had ever had, probably ever would have and I wanted to enjoy it until the utmost, until the umpteenth time, until I could not take anymore, until my body would not take anymore. Until I exhausted. Until they were exhausted.

I felt Wes's lips on mine and he was kissing me, sucking the life right out of me, like he couldn't get enough. We kept fucking, slamming into each other and Zack was sucking and biting at my neck and Wes's hands and mouth were on my tits, biting at them until I threw my head back and came in a rush. It was all over me, all this sensation and my body was in a flush, a red hot flush from the pleasure. It was all over me, the pleasure, just like their hands were all over me. It was forcing me to succumb to it and to eat it and take it for everything it was worth. I couldn't stop coming. I kept coming and coming and just as I thought I was done, it would come back at me stronger, with just a slight more intensity that kept me hanging on until the next sputter.

But it didn't last forever. If it had of, I might have collapsed. I did collapse just after they both came and were pulling away from me, breathing heavily, trying to get their senses back. It took me a good five minutes before I could even utter a word and then the only thing I could say was, "Damn."

Tony yelled, "You never did that with me!"

"So what?" I said offhandedly. "You never did it with me either."

"You never asked me to!"

I sighed and stared at my fingernails, then said, "Whatever."

"How could you?" he asked. "I mean, *how could you?*"

"Tony, you hypocrite. You divorced me, remember?"

"Yeah, but you weren't this worldly woman then."

"Maybe you didn't know me all that well."

He grunted, "Maybe you didn't know yourself."

And maybe that was it. I didn't know myself back

then. Maybe I was no nearer to knowing myself now than I was then but I knew one thing, I was having a damn good time.

"You need to marry one of them," he said.

"You're not getting out of paying alimony, Tony."

"I mean, I just don't think you can do that."

"Do what?" I asked.

"Have two boyfriends at the same time."

I rolled my eyes.

"You know," he said. "You're getting turned out."

"What's that?"

"When a woman starts enjoying sex, she starts wanting it all the time."

I thought about that. Maybe he was right. Maybe I was getting turned out. But I knew it was just my dirty thirties.

"Why couldn't you get turned out when we were together?" he asked.

I stared at the phone and wondered why I still called him. He really got on my nerves sometimes.

"Fuck off, Tony," I said and hung up on him.

Two-times over.

I wanted my fun, but I didn't let my boys "run" over me. I wasn't a doormat. It was all in good fun. I was having the time of my life. I was in La La Land most of the time. My clients at the gym even noticed. I wasn't as much of hard-ass as I had been before.

"Only ten lunges?" Sara, whom I'd been training

for years, asked. "Are you sure?"

I nodded and smiled at her. Then I realized what I'd just done. "No, I was just kidding. Give me fifty."

She started to do it then said, "What about pushups?"

I was already back in La La Land when she said this. I muttered, "Give me five."

"Five?"

"No," I snapped. "Forty."

"Girl pushups?" she asked hopefully.

"You know better than that."

She groaned and got to it. I looked across the room to see Zack, who had suddenly appeared, He smiled at me. I smiled back and he came over and said, "I just dropped by to take you to lunch."

"Great," I said. "We're almost through here."

"Not quite," Sara muttered and lunged.

"Ten more, Sara," I said.

"Bitch," she muttered.

"Just do it," I said and turned to Zack. "It'll be a few minutes."

"Okay," he said and kissed my cheek. "I have a few calls to make, so I'll be in the car when you're ready."

I smiled at him and then he walked back out of the gym.

"Done!" Sara exclaimed, and then rubbed her thigh. "That hurts."

"Do your pushups," I said.

She leaned over and whispered in my ear, "Is it just me or do I detect that you have a new boyfriend?"

I just stared at her and said, "Something like that."

She smiled at me and said, "Go ahead and leave. I'll finish up on my own."

"No, I can't do that."

"Do it for me," she said. "Go on."

"Promise me you'll finish your sets?"

"I promise."

"Really?" I asked.

"Yeah."

"Gee, thanks Sara," I said and patted her shoulder. "I owe you one."

She stared after Zack and said, "Just tell me where to get one like that."

"I got him from a factory," I said. "But his model's been discontinued."

She laughed and said, "Just go."

I raced into the bathroom and changed, then raced out to Zack's SUV and then we were off to a little diner down the street. Once we had ordered, Zack said, "I have a surprise for you."

"Oh great," I said and leaned over and kissed his cheek. "I love surprises. What is it?"

"I want to take you to Hawaii," he said.

"Really?" I squealed. "I've never been to Hawaii."

"Well, you're going now," he said, smiling. "You know, I used to surf a lot. I want to teach you and Hawaii has the best waves."

"Cool," I said. "But I'll have to check with Wes first."

"Oh," he said casually. "I already have."

"Excuse me?"

"I already got it cleared with him," he said and gave

me a big, old smile. "He's cool with it."

He was? *What the hell?*

"But you didn't even ask me first," I said defensively.

"Well, it's not like I *wasn't* going to ask you," he replied and took a sip of his coke. "Why are you mad?"

I crossed my arms and hissed, "Because you two are going around behind my back talking about me."

"Well, it's all good, baby," he said and nodded. "We both think you're the best."

I glared at him. "I don't give a shit. It's like you're becoming best friends. I feel ganged up on."

"We're not ganging up on you," he said and shook his head. "Why are you pissed?"

"I don't know," I snapped. "But I am."

The waitress just then slapped our plates down on the table. I ignored her and lit a cigarette.

"You know," Zack said and shook a bottle of steak sauce. "You're taking this way too seriously."

"I'm taking this way too seriously?" I asked and thought about it. Oh, shit I was. What was wrong with me? Maybe because of them talking without me around made me feel I was losing some of the control in the relationship. I didn't know. Maybe it was just PMS.

"Yes, you are," he said and sighed. "Now, let's get this straight. We're going to Hawaii and you're going to let up on the bitching."

"You're pushing your luck, buddy."

He just stared at me. "I'm serious. Let up a little, would you?"

"I'll consider it."

120

Of course, I went to Hawaii. I wasn't about to turn down a free trip.

It was great. Zack taught me how to surf—i.e. how to fall off a board and into the water without drowning myself. We went to a luau. We frolicked in the sand and drank mai tai's. Then we'd make our way back to our room and have all this hot, island sex. Sex with him in Hawaii was some of the best we'd had.

We'd just finished doing just that when he turned to me and said, "I'm going to surf the pipeline tomorrow."

"What?"

"The pipeline," he said. "It's this enormous wave."

"Yeah, I know, I saw a thing about it on TV," I said and studied him. "It's an enormous wave that can get you killed. Even professionals say it's dangerous."

He nodded. "I've always been a daredevil."

"Or an idiot."

"Wanna come?"

"Hell no," I said and shook my head. "I do not want to witness your demise."

"You're not going to witness my demise?" he said and laughed. "Where do you come up with this shit?"

"Don't know."

He leaned over and kissed me. "Are you sure you don't want to come? It'll be fun."

I leaned back and stared at him. "And please tell me how *that* would be fun."

He shrugged. "Just would be."

"I don't think you should do it."

"Why not?"

"Because it's stupid," I said. "And I'll be by myself all day tomorrow."

"You can come."

"Don't want to."

"Ah," he said and grabbed my hand. "Come with me."

I shook my head. "You can go by yourself."

So he did, leaving me asleep in the early morning. I awoke disoriented and stared around the room until I figured out where I was. Then I fell back to sleep for another three or four hours.

I didn't really have any plans so I took a long shower and ordered room service, and then ate on the terrace. I stared out at the ocean and wondered why I, of all people, was so lucky. I had two—not one but two—great men, a great job, a great house and a great life. Here I was on a great vacation. Well, if Zack came back in one piece, it would be a great vacation.

How did I get so damn lucky? What did I do to deserve all this? Well, for one thing, I took a chance. I smiled, thinking about our last threesome. Now that had been nice. We were all so turned on, it was like we would never be sated, but then we were and I fell asleep between them. When I awoke, Zack was gone and had left a note, "See you soon." Wes was still cuddled up next to me.

I was one lucky bitch. I just was. I should just accept it and go about my business. I stared out at the beach. That was my business. No worries today.

Hopefully, Zack would be okay and then I would see Wes first thing day after tomorrow and then my normal life would resume.

Would it always be like this?

I almost panicked at the thought if it not being. What if they both left me? What if I got bored with them? What if? What if? What if? So fucking what? That was life. Things changed, people changed, and the world stayed the same. Not much you can do about it.

I got ready and headed down to the beach wearing my big, floppy beach hat. I settled in a lounge chair and took a deep breath. Hawaii had to be the most perfect place on Earth.

I lay there for a while until this guy came by and sat down in the chair next to mine. He gave me a little smile before settling back and closing his eyes. I smiled back and turned over. But then, I realized he looked familiar. I turned back around and I'll be damned. It was Trey Ellison! The movie star! He was sitting right next to me!

I turned back to check and sure enough, it was him. Oh. My. God.

"Hot out here, isn't it?" he asked without opening his eyes.

I mumbled something, I don't even know what it was. I think, it was, "Uh, uh...umm..."

He smiled and squinted at me. "I'm Trey."

Yes, you are.

"Who are you?" he asked and shielded his eyes.

"Katrina," I managed to get out without stuttering.

"Nice to meet you."

"And you," I said as casually as I could. *Trey Ellison was sitting right next to me!*

"Would you like some lunch?" he asked. "I was just going to grab a bite."

I stared at him and bit my lip before I responded, "I would like that very much."

We went to the hotel restaurant and everyone made a big fuss over him. I just sat there and smiled, star-struck. Trey Ellison and I were eating lunch together!

We made mild chitchat and he told me a few things that weren't very interesting about himself. He was from Indiana and he was this and he was that. I just sat there admiring and when our food arrived, I couldn't eat. He ate heartily and even reached over and ate some of my food.

"Oh, you can have it," I said and pushed my plate over to him. "I'm not hungry."

"I see that," he said and picked up a French fry. "How do you like Hawaii?"

"I love it," I said and couldn't get over the fact that I was sitting there with him. Trey Ellison! Trey Ellison was buying me lunch! How fucking cool was that?!

"Me too," he said. "I could live here. Where are you from?"

"I live in Vegas."

"Now that's a great place, isn't it?" he asked and chuckled. "I love to play in the old part, on Fremont Street."

I nodded and smiled.

He leaned in close to me and said, "Now I might

have to make a point to get to Vegas more often."

Did he just say that?!

"You're not taken, are you?" he asked.

I just stared at him.

"A girl like you is always taken," he said knowingly. "Right?"

I smiled shyly and muttered, "I am, actually." I didn't say, two-times over. Yeah, I was taken, two-times over. He didn't need to know that.

"Figures."

I couldn't help but grin like a fool at him.

"Wanna come up to my room for a drink?" he asked.

I stared at him and got his meaning immediately. Why not say, *Wanna come up to my room for a fuck?*

I felt that simply nodding was the best answer. Sure, why not? I knew he did shit like this all the time but I couldn't help but follow him upstairs. I don't know why, I just did it. When he handed me a drink, I took it and sipped it, feeling nervous and wondering what the hell I was doing. I didn't have to wonder long because he took the glass out of my hand and kissed me. Just like that.

His kiss was soft; it wasn't fiery like I expected it to be. Nevertheless, it felt good and soon I found myself responding to him, going with him as he led me over to the bed and pushed me back on it.

I shoved everything out of my mind, even though I felt a little weird about doing it with him. Why shouldn't I enjoy it? But for some reason, I couldn't relax enough to. I knew it was guilt. I knew I was

125

cheating on my guys and I knew it was wrong. I should just get up and leave.

"Relax," he said and moved over me.

"No, I really need to—"

"Shh," he murmured and kissed me. "Just relax, baby."

I nodded and tried to. I felt out of myself as he undressed me and kissed me all over. It was only when he pulled my legs apart did I finally start to get into it. I closed my eyes and felt him moving down there, between my legs, kissing and licking at me. All of a sudden, nothing mattered but him kissing and licking at me.

I couldn't take it anymore. I wanted him to fuck me. I pulled him up and kissed him and he shoved his hard cock into me. I smiled a little as he began to move, realizing that he wasn't that great, that I was probably a better lover than he was. I could show him a few things, if I wanted to but for some reason, I didn't really want to. Maybe it was because this was more of a novelty, the pleasure of fucking someone like him.

"You are so hot," he muttered as he fucked me.

I nodded and began to move. I'd at least show him what a good fuck was because, apparently, he didn't know. As I moved, he stared at me, then smiled as I wrapped my legs around his waist. I sucked him into me and clamped my mouth on top of his. He responded by grunting and holding my head still as we kissed.

I kept moving and he slowed down to let me move. I ran my hands through his hair and really began to grind against him. He was having trouble holding it, I could tell, so I let everything go and just concentrated on myself. I might as well get an orgasm.

And I did. As soon as I let myself go, it came at me, tickled me and then burst. I moaned with it as it hit me and he was pumping into me, fucking me with everything he had. He gave one last thrust and it was all over for him. He filled me up and then he collapsed on my chest, breathing heavily.

"Wow," he muttered. "Now that was hot."

I nodded, wishing he'd get the fuck off me. He didn't. He turned and kissed my cheek, then pressed his next to mine. What the hell was that about?

"We should do that again," he said and propped himself up on his elbow to stare at me.

I nodded lamely, feeling a little weird. What had I just done? I'd fucked Trey Ellison! I was a star-fucker! I had fucked a star. That's what I'd just done. I had starfucked. Is this was groupies felt? If so, I was never going to be a groupie. I was feeling a little weird, then I realized it was just guilt. And the guilt was going to eat me alive.

"Just give me a minute," he said and kissed my cheek again. "And we'll do it again."

Like *hell* we would.

"I'll be right back," he said and got up and went into the bathroom.

As soon as the bathroom door closed, I jumped up and pulled on my clothes and ran all the way back to my room, feeling weird about what had just happened. Feeling weird about what it meant.

I stayed in the room all afternoon by myself,

flipping channels on the TV. I was in one of the most beautiful places on earth but I couldn't force myself out of that room. I was at odds with what had just happened and it bothered me because I should have enjoyed it more. But I realized I didn't because I was being used and you don't usually enjoy things when someone's using you. But Trey had really been into it. Well, good for him.

And that's why I enjoyed Wes and Zack so much. We weren't using each other. Each experience was unique and different. We were playing and having fun and experiencing each other. And that's what made it different.

I realized I didn't have to fuck anyone else. Having fucked Trey Ellison was enough to teach me that. I had everything I wanted and could ever need with my boys. I was one lucky bitch. I really was.

Zack came back before six looking exhausted.

"How did it go?" I asked and grinned at him, happy to see he was all in one piece. And glad he had come back early so I could distract myself from the thoughts of what'd I'd done earlier.

"I didn't do it," he said sadly.

"You didn't? Why?"

He looked at the wall and said, "I didn't want to meet my demise."

I grinned and walked over to him, pulled his lips down on mine and once they made that initial contact, I knew Trey Ellison would be nothing in my memory but a sad mistake. This, what we had, was something. Something I never wanted to lose.

Coming home.

When I got back, Wes was waiting on me at my house. He jumped on me and fucked me before I could even get out a hello.

"God," he murmured. "I've missed you so much, baby."

"I missed you, too," I said and stared into his eyes as we fucked. "I've missed this."

He grinned and took my face in his hands and kissed me. "I love you so much."

"I love you, too," I said and arched away from the bed. "I love fucking you so much."

"Whenever I fuck you," he muttered. "It's like coming home. I get homesick when you go away."

"Mmm," I moaned and grabbed his face, kissing him. "I've missed you, too."

He began to eat at my lips, at my face and at my breasts. I lay there and squirmed against him, sucking him into me. I loved the heaviness of his body on mine. I thought briefly about Trey Ellison collapsing on me. I shuddered with guilt and pushed him out of my mind and concentrated back on Wes, who was so far gone, I had to catch up or there'd be nothing left for me.

I wrapped my legs around his waist and pressed against him. Soon we were slapping up against each other, as our fucking took over our bodies. We held onto it for a long time, just enjoying the sensation, and then I felt the orgasm.

"Oh, God, yeah!" I cried and felt it grip me and rip through my body. "Ahhhh… YEAHHHH!"

He was close behind. He pounded into me and I felt his hot cum fill me. I moaned and licked at his face and then he collapsed on top of me and was quiet. I kissed his temple and pressed my face next to his.

Phew. That was quick. I'd been home less than five minutes and I had already been laid. I'd have to go away more often if this was what I was going to get.

"Next time," he said, pulling back to stare into my eyes. "We all go and we get two separate rooms."

I grinned. "And I can scurry back and forth?"

"Yeah," he said but then his smiled dropped. "How long is this thing going to last?"

"What do you mean?"

"I mean," he said and sighed. "How long with this threesome or ménage a trois or whatever it's called… How long before… You know?"

I didn't know. It couldn't last forever. Things like this didn't last. They never did. I mean, you never hear of anyone being in a relationship with two guys and having divine threesomes. I'd never even heard of it even happening at all. I guess we were just unique. Or we didn't know much about how other people lived.

"It'll last," I said and smoothed the hair back from his forehead. "Until one of us gets bored with it or one of us doesn't want to do it anymore. That's how long it will last."

He nodded, liking my answer. "Okay. I was just wondering."

I smiled and kissed him, pulling him back on top of me, opening my legs to him, myself up to him, missing the way his cock filled me and feeling whole once it was replaced.

"God, I love you," he said and began to fuck me. "I love you so much."

"I love you, too," I said and moaned, kissing and licking at his face and neck. "I love you so, so much."

He fucked me for a moment, then held my head still and forced me to look into his eyes. He resumed like that, fucking me, taking me, staring into my eyes, not letting them waver for one second. He had me then and he knew it. And I had him and I had the world and I loved it. I loved having everything I had and wanting all of it, being glad that this was where I was at that exact moment, being glad to be alive.

"Let's stay like this forever," he said. "You and me."

I nodded and felt him, all of him at that moment in time. And then I felt a pang of guilt. Guilt because I had cheated on him and on Zack. It didn't mean anything. I could have done without it but then I had done it, mostly due in part to see if I *could* do it.

"Wes," I said. "I need to tell you something."

"Shh," he said and fucked me, grinding himself into me. "Just feel it."

I pushed all thoughts out of my head and felt what he was giving me then. I felt all of it, all of the love he had for me and because of that feeling, I began to come, I began to orgasm and it was a sweet one, a sweet one that was a little bitter because I had done something I shouldn't have.

He was coming too and as he came, he moaned a deep moan that told me he loved me and that what we were doing was more important than anything else we could ever do. We were giving ourselves to each other and because of that nothing else mattered, nor would it ever matter.

So I decided to keep my big mouth shut.

Honesty.

Of course, I wrestled with it for days. I would decide to tell them, and then would decide against it, and then I would go crazy for a few minutes before I always came to the exact same conclusion: I didn't know what I was going to do.

So I kept my mouth shut, decided that was the best thing to do. But I felt, in a way, I had betrayed them. On the surface, it really wasn't that big a deal. But underneath, it was eating me alive.

I knew I was wrestling with it because I was having so much fun with them. I knew something bad might happen if I told them and maybe I was setting myself up for failure. Maybe I didn't want to be happy. Maybe I couldn't stand it. Why did I deserve all this? What was so special about me anyway?

It was guilt, pure and simple guilt. I hated it and tried to shake it off and get back to the moment, but I couldn't. I knew I was punishing myself. Punishing myself because, I suppose, it was time. I'd been happy for too long. I'd been content and blissful and that stuff can't last forever. Something had to ruin it. I suppose I was the one who was going to ruin it for myself.

This went on for days until I decided I would tell

them. I wanted to tell them because… Because I was part fool and part optimist. I thought if I told them, we could all laugh it off. And then, I could move on from it. I could free myself just by being honest.

But then I remembered Wes's extreme reaction when he'd found out about Zack and me. I didn't want a repeat of that. And what would Zack do? He might throw something through the window. Even though he was extremely laid back, he wasn't laid back when it came to me. He was very protective and once when we were out and this guy accidentally pushed me, he threatened to kick his ass until the guy backed away apologizing.

No way was I telling them. Fuck 'em. It would be my secret and eventually I'd get over the guilt. Until then, I'd suffer in silence. I was never cheating again. I wasn't built for it.

A few days after we got back from Hawaii, I invited them both over for dinner and then a little later on, a little something-something. And then after that, we could do it again.

After we'd finished eating and were sitting around sipping wine and talking, the phone rang. Wes got up to answer it. I didn't bat an eye because he always answered the phone at my house and I always answered it at his. It was just one of those couple things we did.

"Hello," he said.

"Oh," Zack said and leaned over towards me. "I forgot to tell you that you packed a pair of your shorts into my suitcase."

"Why didn't you bring them?" I asked and sipped my wine.

"I forgot until now," he said. "I'll get them to you tomorrow or the next day."

I nodded and glanced at Wes, who was on the phone, a look of consternation on his face. He turned to me and his eyes narrowed. I sat up taller and asked, "Who is it?"

He turned away from me and said, "Yes, this is her house. Who is this again?"

What was going on?

"Who?" he asked. "I don't understand. What? Who am I? I'm her fiancé. Who are you? Huh? Her what?"

He turned to stare at me. I suddenly realized what was happening and what was about to unfold. I sunk down in my seat. Oh, no. This couldn't be happening to me! Not again!

"And why are you calling her?" he asked, still staring at me. "Oh, really? You met in Hawaii? Is that so? Huh. Can you talk to her? Yeah. Hold on."

I almost reached for the phone, but he didn't hand it to me. He hung it up and then turned on me, a look of fury in his eyes.

"Why the hell is Trey Ellison calling you?" he snapped.

I sunk down deeper in my seat, wishing I could just disappear. I decided to play dumb. "What do you mean? Trey Ellison? That must have been a joke. I bet it was Tony."

"It wasn't Tony," he said. "It was Trey Ellison. Why is he calling you?"

Stonewall, girl! Stone-fucking-wall!

"Katrina?" he asked.

I shrugged. "I bet it was Nick, from the gym. He's such a hoot! Pretending to be Trey Ellison! I'll get him for this!"

"Trey Ellison the movie star?" Zack asked looking at me. "I heard he was in our hotel when we were in Hawaii…"

I watched his face at it dawned on him.

"…oh," he muttered. "Oh."

One, two, three. Now all the pieces to the puzzle were in place. Thanks, Trey, you lousy fuck!

Zack stood up and pointed at me. "You fucked him!"

I jumped up and said, "No, I didn't!"

"Then why did he say you two were 'old lovers'?" Wes asked.

"Because we… We, uh… When I was a cocktail waitress, he was at the casino one night and—"

"Shut up," Wes said, shaking his head. "If you're going to lie, at least try."

"You were a cocktail waitress?" Zack asked.

"No, she wasn't!" Wes snapped. "Katrina, did you fuck him?"

I stared at Wes, then at Zack, then at my feet. I nodded lamely.

"You fucked him," Wes asked and shook his head at me like a teacher. "I can't believe you fucked him."

"He was just one guy," I said.

"One guy?" Zack said. "Aren't we enough for you?"

"Of course you are!" I exclaimed and suddenly felt

defensive. "Why are you two so mad?"

They just stared at me, fuming.

"It wasn't that great," I said. "He was really terrible in the sack."

"Like that makes what you did better," Wes snapped.

"Come on, guys," I begged. "Just forget about it."

"Let me ask you this," Zack said. "What if one of us fucked some other girl?"

My stomach bottomed out. Okay, I know I was one big hypocrite but it did make me sick. I said honestly, "I wouldn't want to know."

"See!?" Wes exclaimed. "Now you know how we feel! Why did you have to give him your number?"

"I didn't!" I exclaimed. "I swear I didn't give him my number. I never even told him my last name! I don't know how he got it!"

"Whatever," Wes said.

"Wes—" I began.

He threw his hand up at me, grabbed his jacket and left the house quietly. I wanted to run after him but I couldn't. Mainly because I knew he didn't want me to. He didn't want to see me just then, maybe not ever.

Zack let out a sigh and stood up from the table. He wasn't looking at me either.

"Zack," I said. "It didn't mean anything."

"No," he said. "It might not have but I thought we had something special and I just don't think that anymore."

"But why?" I cried. "It didn't mean anything!"

He turned on me and yelled, "So does that mean I

136

don't mean anything either?!"

"No, of course not!"

"Well, that's how I feel," he said and glared at me.

"I'm sorry," I said. "I'm just so sorry."

"Whatever," he said. "You trying to get a foursome going now?"

"No!" I exclaimed. "Zack, please, just stay and listen to me!"

He shook his head and went to the door. "I don't want to hear it. See you later."

"Zack!" I called after him. "Zack, don't leave!"

But he was gone.

I wanted to fall to the floor and die. Instead I fell to the floor and couldn't move. I just couldn't move. There was nowhere to go and nothing to do. I had lost everything.

Damn Trey Ellison anyway. He was my undoing!

Love, love and love.

They broke up with me. Both of them out the damn door. Who could blame them? *I* could blame them, that's who! I mean, come on, aren't we allowed at least one mistake?

I guess not.

I was devastated. What could I do to get them back? Apparently nothing. Neither would return my phone calls.

I knew I had fucked something really good up but how was I supposed to know they'd both react in that way? Maybe I was asking for too much. Maybe I was being *too* selfish. Maybe I didn't understand it was all about the love. The love I felt for Wes and the love I felt for Zack and the love I felt for myself. I did feel love for myself. I wouldn't have done any of that if I hadn't. It's good to love yourself. Even better when someone loves you back.

Maybe I had fucked it up on purpose. Maybe it was all about guilt, about loving too much, about getting too much out of life. Maybe I felt like I didn't deserve it. And that's why I had ruined it.

They let me stew in my own juices for a few days. I was about insane with needing them. So much I was going to get on my knees and grovel, beg, plead, do anything to get them back. At least one of them. But they both cut me out.

Tony said, "Well, since you're free now, why don't we get back together?"

"You've got to me kidding me," I said and rolled my eyes.

"No," he said. "I mean, why not? We were good together once, we can be good again."

"Tony?" I said.

"Yes?"

"You don't have a fucking clue," I said and hung up on him.

Then Wes came by one day and he wanted me back. I almost fell over. I was so happy, I cried as he hugged me.

"You made a mistake," he said. "I can forgive you for it."

I smiled at him. "Thanks."

"No problem," he said and pulled me over to the couch. "I want to ask you something."

"What is it?"

"I want to know," he said. "If you still want to get married."

I stared at him. Uh, uh... *what?!*

"I was just thinking about that is all," he said. "I mean why not? We've been through a lot and we've made it. Marriage isn't so scary when you know you can make it."

He was right. But... But... Yeah. But what?

"I'll think about it," I said.

"Please do," he told me and kissed the tip of my nose. "I really want to do it this time. And I want to buy you a new wedding dress."

I nodded and grinned at him. "Okay."

"And it can just be us, you know?" he said. "Me and you, like it was before. We're so good together."

I nodded. We were. I giggled and pressed my nose to his. "I am so glad you came back."

"Me too." He pulled back and stared into my eyes. "I knew the threesome thing wouldn't last forever, and that's okay, baby. We can always pick up another guy, if you like, before we get married."

And after we get married? No more threesomes, that's what. That's what he was saying. It would be okay before but after, not so much.

"It doesn't have to be Zack," he said.

A pain shot through my chest. But I wanted Zack! I didn't want some other guy. It wouldn't be the same. I wanted him! But then again, he didn't want me. Not anymore. Wes was right. It might just be better for me and him to be together by ourselves. I hated that but Zack didn't want me anymore. All because of Trey Ellison. Maybe it wasn't because of Trey Ellison. Maybe it was because he was looking for a reason to get out.

Well, now he had it.

Wes started to kiss me just as the phone rang. I pulled back and stared at him. He shrugged and I got up to answer it.

When I picked up, Zack said, "It's me. I've been going crazy thinking about what an idiot I've been. I have to see you."

I couldn't believe my luck. This couldn't be happening. But it was and it was all too easy. There had to be a catch. But if there was a catch, I didn't want to know about it for a long time. I just wanted to get back into the groove and do what I did best, which was fucking.

I knew the catch. The catch was marrying Wes. But maybe I could postpone it a little and we could do a few more threesomes. And then we could get married and it would all be over. But I didn't want to lose Zack either. I knew one day I would have to choose. I would just wait until that day.

Maybe we wouldn't go on as we did. Maybe they would grow apart from me and find someone else or maybe I would. But right now, right this day, I had both of them and that was better than good enough.

"I'm glad to hear from you," I said to Zack and then smiled at Wes. My smiled widened as I realized I was going to get what I wanted and whatever that happened to be, it was the best feeling in the whole world. I couldn't stop smiling. For apparent reasons. I was one lucky bitch.

Zack sighed and said, "I was thinking…"

"Yeah?" I asked and smiled.

"I was thinking," he said and drew a breath. "That you…"

"Uh huh."

"That you and me… God, I've never said anything like this to anyone."

"What is it?" I asked and glanced at Wes, who was staring at me. He smiled. I smiled back.

"I'll just spit it out."

"Okay," I said.

"I think we should get married," he said hurriedly, then, "Oh, that wasn't so bad."

Did he just… No. He didn't just say that.

"What do you think?" he asked like this was the best idea he'd ever had.

What did I think? I'll tell you. It was the worst idea I'd ever heard! What was wrong with these men? Didn't they know that they'd given me a taste of candy and were now taking it away from me? Didn't they care that I loved our threesomes? I knew once I got hitched with one of them, then threesome land would be over. Things would change. It wasn't fair!

"I mean, the threesomes are great and whatever," he said. "But me and you, baby, that's what I want.

Maybe later on, we can try that again."

"Uh…" I muttered. "Uh…"

"And Wes is a great guy," he said. "Don't get me wrong, but I just want… I just want it to be us."

I stared at Wes. He'd said the same thing.

"Katrina?" he asked. "What do you think?"

The gig was up. The gig was definitely up. It was over. And now I was even more fucked than I had been before. Damn it. So much for being lucky. I stared at Wes and got an idea. Why not? I didn't have anything to lose. If I could just get them both in the same room then we could all talk and then maybe they wouldn't make me choose, not just yet. We could also do something else to take our minds off it. And that something else was what I wanted. At least one more time. One last time and then we'd all move on.

"Uh, Zack," I said. "Why don't you come over and we can discuss it in a little more detail?"

CPSIA information can be obtained at www.ICGtesting.com
Printed in the USA
LVOW092146110612

285677LV00001B/6/A